FOOL'S BLOODING

When young thugs burst into the home of writer Richard Kind, taking himself and his family hostage, it seems as though the world has come to an end. Instead of fiction, he faces a bitter reality in which all things are possible – imprisonment, rape, even murder ...

Tension grows as the hours pass and a story unfolds of an incredible, bungled crime which has led the men to Kind's door. These are not professional criminals, it seems, merely youngsters frightened out of their wits by events which Kind can only glimpse.

In an atmosphere taut with violence, Kind faces his own cowardice and his wife's contempt.

But Kind has an ace in the hole: a small paperknife, concealed in his pocket – a simple object which assumes greater and greater significance as Kind lays plans to recapture his freedom and the book approaches its final, bloody end ...

FOOL'S BLOODING

PETER PIKE

ROBERT HALE · LONDON

©Peter Pike 1984
First published in Great Britain 1984

ISBN 0 7090 1719 7

Robert Hale Limited
Clerkenwell House
Clerkenwell Green
London EC1R 0HT

Photoset in North Wales by
Derek Doyle & Associates, Mold, Clwyd
Printed in Great Britain by
St Edmundsbury press,
Bury St Edmunds, Suffolk.
Bound by Woolnough Bookbinding Limited

One

Later, Richard Kind was unable to explain the instinct which made him reach out for the paper-knife.

Seconds before, he had been absorbed in a short story he was writing for a woman's magazine. It was a good story, he believed. Emotional but quite sharp and with enough integrity to keep Kind from feeling embarrassed by it. He was almost prepared to put his real name to this one, though normally he used girls' names for the magazines.

He had finished the first script and was rewriting, putting the piece into a more readable form. He would type several words, clattering them out on the typewriter with an intense speed which sounded like one continuous noise, and then he would pause and gaze out of the window in front of his desk. This was a habit.

There were trees in the distance: elms and some oaks, moving in the small morning breeze. They mesmerized him for a while, soothed feelings of impatience at the slowness of his work. Kind enjoyed the sight very much and had to force himself to look elsewhere, often had to do that …

Slightly to the left, a stiff old man worked among the greenery of a long, thin garden. Straight in front, Kind could see the kitchen roof of the house at the back, and beyond that the large brick face of the biggest detached house in the area. Sometimes he saw women in uniform at the windows of this house – air hostesses possibly; occasionally these women would pause, look up at the converted bedroom which Kind used as an office, and stare. He would smile, but they were too far away to see.

He wrote: "She had never experienced love and regretted the absence of its pain – for she was sure that love was pain, must be to have caused so much distress in the world."

Was this right?

He hesitated, unsure whether to throw away the sheet of paper and start again. It was almost right but something seemed false, seemed contrived, and Kind disliked that. Knew that he ran a constant risk of sentimentality in these stories and that later – an hour after writing, a day perhaps – this would cause him great anguish, much embarrassment.

So, was this right?

Directly before him on the desk lay three large piles of paper: one rough, for first drafts, one fine for top copies and one flimsy for the carbons. To the right of these piles were three books: *Chambers Dictionary, Brewers Dictionary of Phrase and Fable,* and *Roget's Thesaurus.* From time to time as he sat and wrote day after day, Kind would reach for one of these books and browse for a while; sometimes he became lost like this for half an hour at a time and would suddenly remember his duty (his wife and child, his bank balance) and put away the book and start writing again – the novel or perhaps another short story. It was, he always told friends, a hard life; harder than he had imagined.

To the right of the books was a sharp metal spike vicious enough to go through flesh (had once: there was a tiny scar on Kind's right hand to prove it). Many ideas and half-finished stories ended up on this spike, pieces overrun by sentiment or a mawkish plot, and Kind would jab them to extinction with great power, enjoying the reluctance of the pages to be penetrated. The spike was almost full. The story he was writing would probably not end up here.

Just in front of the spike was a series of joined, upright

tubes forged out of red plastic, and in these Kind kept his paper-clips, pencils, pens, rubbers and also his paper-knife.

It was a good paper-knife. It was made out of one continuous piece of thin, flexible stainless steel with a tubular handle expanding from pencil-thinness to that of a crayon, the sort young children use at school. Its blade, which was mirror-shiny, began with a triangular shape just after the hilt, swiftly flattening into a thin stiletto upon which was faintly inscribed the name of the manufacturing company: Tolcodron. The whole blade was perhaps three and a half inches long, the handle about four.

Sometimes when he wrote, Kind would pause and draw the paper-knife from the longest plastic tube and play absent-mindedly with it – not doing so for long because he knew from experience that this could become an absorbing activity – bouncing the blade on the desk top, flexing it between fingers or just putting it to his face and feeling the coolness, the blunt-sharpness of it. The point was almost evilly sharp, the sides simply thin. Kind would put the thing away after only a short time and begin typing again, a little disturbed by the pleasure to be had from handling the slim weight of it. Sometimes, he wondered if paper-knives were not simply executive toys, invented to prop up the macabre, day-dreaming instincts of those whose lives centred upon desks and sheaves of white paper. He never used it for cutting. Never opened letters with it. Where had he got it? He wasn't sure; perhaps a Christmas gift. He doubted that he would have bought such a thing for himself.

Kind decided to let the original sentence stand, and began looking at what followed: "Perhaps it was a sweet pain, she told herself; love – a glorious suffering."

He began typing.

It was at this moment that his wife called from

downstairs, and because the typewriter was running at
speed he only heard her as a sound at first. He had to stop
and shout, "What?" loudly, without turning round or
taking his eyes from the words.

Her voice came again, more clearly this time.

"Can you come down a minute please?"

Kind half turned his head towards the door behind him
and frowned. Normally, Jo tried never to bother him
when he was working – they needed what little money his
writing brought in and she respected the fragility of his
concentration; it seemed odd that she should call out to
him in this way. Beyond that, whenever Jo did need to
disturb him she would speak from just outside the door
and not shout up the stairs. This was what made Kind
frown; also the tone of her voice which had seemed quite
serious – almost subdued; so quiet in fact that he had not
heard her clearly at first.

Still caught in that delicate world between imagination
and the first touch of reality, Kind was disturbed by the
changes. He experienced one brief, absurd feeling of fear
and he shouted back quickly, "What is it?"

There was a silence.

Why a silence?

Kind was about to repeat his shout when Jo's voice
came again. "Could you just come, please? Quickly."

The fear returned to Kind. It was partly imaginary,
drawn from the coloured fictional world which lay at his
fingertips, but also was a worry born of broken patterns.
Their current life had evolved over almost a year, its form
had hardened and set and there were these rules to break
now. In a way, some of them had just been broken: a
subdued call from downstairs, a quieter repetition.

Kind shouted, "Right. Coming."

It was at this moment, as he stood up, still frowning,
that the unfathomed instinct which he later forgot made
him reach into the red plastic tube and draw from it the

small, slim paper-knife which was the only weapon he could possibly have to hand.

He hesitated, then tucked it inside his jeans at the back, just under the loose overshirt where it could not be seen. It felt cold, insecure and slightly ridiculous.

Yet Kind left the weapon in place as he turned, moved the cushion which kept the door closed (the handle had broken years before, Kind had never bothered to mend it though Jo often asked him to) and walked out onto the landing.

To the right there was a small window looking down onto their tiny, dishevelled side-street. A woman was pushing an old bicycle up the hill away from the house, and beyond her a pensioner whom he knew as Mr Harris was cutting a hedge with tired movements of the shears.

Straight in front of Kind, the stairs dropped sharply, then turned back on themselves and ran down a few more steps into the hallway. The bannisters were of solid wood and so he was unable to see his wife, who was obviously standing somewhere by the door to the kitchen. It was completely quiet down there. It was not a big house and there would normally have been some noise, not least from their son who was 2 years old and very active. Jo and the boy between them could easily create enough disturbance to ruin Kind's concentration just by sitting in the lounge and playing small, childish games.

Again, he hesitated.

What had made him hide the paper-knife in his jeans? Why, in a normal working morning, did such small signs of change induce fear? Already the knowledge was fading though Kind could still taste the emotion of it.

He was tempted to call out a tentative challenge to his wife, something that would make her respond calmly, with ordinary impatience perhaps, anything to push away the imagined, coloured world which made him feel so odd ...

And yet he said nothing, did not call out at all, and this was because (he realized, beginning the short walk down the first flight of stairs) it would have been embarrassing for him to have revealed his sudden, armed nervousness by shouting for reassurance.

At the stair-turn was another window, set at knee height, providing illumination for the kitchen and part of the angled hallway. Stopping here, looking down, Kind saw at once with only a small shock that his wife was not alone, though he had not heard anyone knock at the door.

He saw men. They seemed to hold ... They seemed to hold guns of some kind; a shotgun, a pistol.

His wife was clutching their son and looking up at him. He was aware of the pale moon of her face, the white set of fear.

Kind felt bewildered.

"What's going on?" he asked.

One of the men – a smallish, untidy-looking person – said, "Get down here. Now." His voice was rough and urgent.

This was unbelievable.

Kind, looking from his wife to the men and then back to Jo, began to get angry.

"Who the hell are you?" he half-shouted. "What the hell do you – "

"Shut it or I shoot!"

A pistol was levelled at Kind's eyes. It shook a little and he suffered a momentary terror which stripped him of anger; even the surprise left him.

Slowly, looking at Jo for an explanation which she seemed too frightened to give, Kind stepped down the final four stairs into the small, crowded hallway. There was a smell of sweat, male sweat, and an intense feeling of claustrophobia.

He had been writing. This was a normal and small

town. There was *no reason* for armed men to be here in his home, to push him like this, to shout, "Get *in* there."

He said, "What is it? What do you want? What is it?"

"I warned you."

The untidy man pushed Kind into the lounge and then pushed Jo, still with Daniel.

Kind said, "Leave them … "

He turned back on the men but then faced the same pistol, the same trembling, frightened threat. He backed away and wondered what was going to happen, what they would do to him, what they would do to his family. This could not happen. This was unreal, surely?

Two

Kind had strong views on characterization. He felt that people were not objects to be described by this action or that expression: they were not what they did while you were looking but what they had done years ago and years before that. They were a total, and sometimes only pieces of a total: parts showing through, being dominant for a while and then being forgotten. This is what he tried to write about. He tried to give glimpses of people as spirits trailing back over years. Sometimes he felt a little fey explaining this because he had not quite got used to being a writer.

A year before the morning when he walked downstairs feeling foolish, being shocked facing armed men in his home, Kind had been working for an insurance company and doing quite well. This was his point. Anyone seeing and describing him then would have labelled him as solid, quite ordinary, slightly dull: different routines, mostly unshakeable. Yet this was not true. He was really not just that but something he had been before, well beyond that point. At times, like everyone else, he could be different and had been.

Kind had served the insurance company for five years, working his way up from a selling job which he had disliked, to a supervisory position where he managed to combine some natural authority with a little directness – hence his popularity among most of those who worked for and with him. The simpler ones said that Kind had the common touch, that he never lorded it; those with more insight recognised that he had enough imagination to use the feelings of those around him.

Five years was an immense time though: significant that he suffered it for so long when the truth he admitted to Jo was that he did not like it that much.

Before that he had been what he still described (over rare dinners with strangers for instance) as a hippy.

It was a title Kind had held only for a while: eighteen months in America, a period which would have been much longer if the immigration authorities had not been adamant that a British national with an expired visa and a pretty but apparently unsupported wife was not a welcome visitor to the country.

Kind had packed his guitar, watered his vegetable patch – rented for almost nothing and which had provided them with potatoes, tomatoes and marijuana – and taken the next available stand-by flight to Heathrow. Jo had cried, Kind merely stared out of the window. But he had enjoyed America and his brief, careless run.

Before this, he had worked for another insurance company, and before that he had been a clerk for the BBC – a job which ended after six months when a studio manager tried to kiss him in the control room of a drama studio during a Sunday shift and Kind hit him once, very accurately. After that, there had seemed no place for him in the BBC and so he left, was unemployed for a while and then, dangerously close to poverty and ignored by his parents, had limped into insurance.

The one consolation attached to this move was that it led to his meeting with Jo.

This happened on a pretty spring day while Kind was cold-selling life insurance and sweating in horror at each anguished moment. He knocked on the door of a promisingly large house on the outskirts of Oxford and a small, slim, dark-haired girl with amused eyes answered and listened to his tired spiel for some minutes before interrupting to say that he was unconvincing. Kind, suddenly aware that life-insurance was peripheral to his meeting with this girl, laughed and told her that he had no insurance himself and did not really believe in it for anything but cars and married men. They had drinks together. Became embarrassingly involved with each other in an acutely short space of time. Married noisily, expensively, with a reception which cost Jo's father more than twelve hundred pounds. (The old man had offered Kind a choice: cash or a lavish party. Surprisingly, Kind had taken the latter and so he and Jo lived in rented accomodation for the first three years of their married life.)

One evening a few months after the wedding, Jo and Kind consumed a bottle of claret and two joints. They lay dazed and holding each other on cushions scented with cheap perfume bought from a pretentious Indian store located among Oxford's less respectable shopping streets. Jo told Kind that she had at last discovered what sort of a person he was. She said, without invitation, "You're half-way between dull and fiery, but not in a normal way. A normal way would be quite normal, like everybody else. A bit of both. You go from one to the other, that's what you're about. You'll plod for ages and then flare up at all that wasted time. You'll not think things out clearly but you'll *know* how people'll feel – I've seen you do it, going on instinct. You're wasted in insurance. I bet you see it one day and get angry. Honestly."

"Rubbish."

"Really?"

The conversation made Kind feel restless, indeed wasted. He neither argued any further nor agreed, simply inhaled smoke and waited for her to press her point but she did not. He offered no explanation of her own character in return and knew that this disappointed her but, for the moment, felt too self-absorbed to make the effort.

Slowly over the following months the two grew into each other. Made small discoveries of the kind Jo had talked about but kept them secret; became comfortable. They were very happy.

When Kind threw up his job and took Jo off to America her parents reacted with furious dignity. Really, Kind was simply fulfilling Jo's prophecy, and perhaps subconsciously he had always been aware that he would do so one day.

On their last night in England they ate a cold, sullen meal with Jo's father and mother (Kind's parents had telephoned good wishes from the West Country without indicating that a visit would be worthwhile). It was the last supper, followed by a small aside as Kind and Jo's father did the washing-up alone.

Scrubbing furiously among a lather of suds the old man said, "Listen – don't get her into any trouble out there."

"No, of course not." (Wiping up.)

"You do and I'll go to any lengths. I'll make you suffer for it."

"She's my wife, Mr Plaistow."

Silence.

Both men were ready to burst into anger but neither

did: the old man was held back by fear of his daughter;
Kind by sympathy – he understood how the old man felt.

They caught an early-hours flight and landed in
torrential rain. Their city rooms were abysmal, the days
hot and grey; neither was sure what they had come for
and each suspected that it was not for this: the grimy
staircase, the brusque rudeness of the fat man behind the
counter in the food store.

They bickered, felt total disenchantment hovering
behind each hot sentence and each early night. The city
baked them, sucked out their freshness and spat clinging
dust at them from shallow gutters. Their lives were
waste-paper scraps, fast hamburgers and a sense of
unease. They were waiting for something but had not a
clue yet as to what it might be. This was America. Kind
had brought his wife here for – something. Something
special, he had not revealed it, was waiting to be told and
sometimes feared that Jo blamed him for this.

They moved further south, out into the country. They
hired a broken-down shack with a patch of scrub land
(which later, under care, gave goods which seemed
splendid, rich). Jo took illicit part-time work at a gas
station and there her English accent introduced her to a
crowd of young men and women in a Volkwagen
minibus. The minibus became very important to them
both. It took them hundreds of shared miles and led
them to sights and sounds which slowly identified
themselves as precisely that unspoken vision which had
lured Kind there in the first place. He never said so, but
both knew, both understood that it was for this – this hot,
brash, laughing America.

The crowd in the minibus were part of a rock group.
Quite good, not outstanding, but they earned money and
let Kind play rhythm on lesser dates where college kids
jumped and Jo stood in the winds and smoked dope with
people who were used to speaking normally at great

volume. Sleeping, drugged and beaten by music in the early hours, they would touch and wake and make love and lie still then talking very slowly and with massive pauses. Jo told him, "This is the fiery part. I told you you could."

Kind wanted to agree, but touched her with his foot and found he had not the energy left.

They gave a party to which over a hundred people came, spilling out beyond the patch of tended land into neighbouring gardens where old men and women threatened to call the cops. They studied yoga, ate macrobiotic food, discussed absurd philosophies with gentle, untutored minds. Grew lean.

Kind took to writing songs, some of which the group played and praised. Then he switched suddenly to a novel which was very bad but filled many nights, many dawn hours when the light was crystal on a borrowed typewriter. He discovered a surprising peace in words and Jo, sensing a change, read the book and declared it good. "You can do it," she said. "You really can. Honestly. Not this one, but you can."

And then the immigration officers called one evening during dinner and the whole edifice crumbled, all the bricks and mortar of life, plunging one by one to the ground. They had to leave. They fought it but lost. Watered the garden. Cried. Flew home to Heathrow and there took a taxi and shivered in the cold. People stared at Kind's long hair and eventually he cut it and got a job with another insurance firm. Jo said nothing but he recognized that this was the other side she had spoken about, the plodding life was about to begin.

In fact, it lasted for five years, five rising years in which they saved money, bought a house in Haywards Heath thirteen miles north of Brighton where the South Coast bathed in pebbled beaches and summer pints of whelks and mild.

Jo gave birth to Daniel and this became a quite distinct, fiery love. Kind watched the boy's delight, his fascinated eyes, and grew to feel obsessed with his own comparative dullness.

Then Jo's father died suddenly, and the angry old man left them three thousand pounds with which, after tears and comforts, they reduced their mortgage to a trickle. Then, pushed by the echo of America days, Kind rediscovered writing and gave in his notice. The firm was grave. Held up warning hands and could not promise to have him back; perhaps he was unsound after all.

Kind gave a decent farewell party and many things were forgiven. They presented him with a tankard for which he had no use but he admired the inscription which read, simply: "To a very decent colleague and friend." Prey to sentimentality, Kind responded with a short, blunt speech because he did not trust himself to say more.

He told Jo he would give it two years and then begin plodding again, and meanwhile there would be not so much fire as friction – the heat of work, of effort. If sheer hours could work the miracle they would do so. He would try very hard. She understood that he was apologizing, smiled and said, "Don't be silly. It's much the best thing."

That was nine months before Kind looked up from his typewriter and felt unreal enough to push a paper-knife into his belt and cover it with his shirt just prior to walking downstairs and being told to come on by men with guns.

Three

The men seemed frightened or perhaps just nervous. Kind was aware of this within moments of being ordered into the lounge. The odd sense of unreality and bewilderment still held him and so his own fear was subdued – a waiting force.

He did as they asked and decided that if the men planned to hurt his wife and child then he would have to begin fighting the moment this became clear. He knew that he was quite a strong man, though at 30 had lost a little natural strength and fitness; he believed he had enough reserves to make a reasonable attack in the brief time he might have before they shot him. Also, he had the paper-knife, which would cut nothing but was fine enough to stab with.

Kind took these decisions in moments, grateful for the absence of real emotion which enabled him to do so.

The man who had first spoken and who ordered them into the lounge now said quickly, "All right, sit down and shut up. Don't say a word."

What was the point of all this?

Kind turned anxiously to his wife and saw that she was holding Daniel with too much force: the child was clutched to her, wide-eyed, attention caught half-way between discomfort and fascination with the men, the two pistols, the shotgun. (All these weapons, all this possibility of death or wounding. Kind felt appalled.) Reaching out, he gently touched Jo's shoulder, trying to reassure her by feel, but she shook once, almost in spasm, and then turned to him as if she wanted *him* to explain, to point out to her what these men were doing in their house. Kind could not. At least though, he noticed, Jo relaxed her hold on Daniel just a little.

Kind pointed to the couch by the far wall of the lounge and they sat together without saying a word.

The moment they were seated, Kind felt his wife's hand reach for his own and hold with surprising strength. Poor Jo. Overwhelmingly now he felt this, and he squeezed her fingers in reply – but this seemed unimportant, she clung to him as she had clung to Daniel: with desperation. He could sense her fear, stronger than the men's, in the wetness of her hand, in the jerking, twitching movements of her fingers. Kind wanted to say something to calm her, wanted this more than anything, but felt that this would be too much of a risk at present.

The men were talking to each other.

The one who had so far given the orders and who seemed to be in charge, said, "You check upstairs. All the rooms – very careful. Go on." He seemed agitated, almost alarmed. Kind watched carefully, trying to concentrate, to understand. One man left the room and as he did so the other shouted, "Don't let anybody see you at the windows. Keep the shooter down."

Shooter. Television words: enormously foreign jargon. Kind opened his mouth to speak – encouraged briefly by the foolishness of words like shooter – but then he shut his mouth again because he knew how unimportant these guns and men made him.

The leader now turned to his remaining companion and said, "You stay here and watch this lot. Not a word – right?" He looked directly at Kind who only nodded. The man left and so only one stood guard, holding a shotgun in an almost theatrically threatening manner, pointed half-way between Kind and his wife.

This man met his eyes, and then looked away, looked to one side, met his eyes, looked away …

He was quite tall and somewhere in his mid-twenties. A lean face, so lean that there were creases in both cheeks which might have been scars but were too tired. He was badly shaven and a black stubble gave his chin and throat an unhealthy, dirty look. Kind noted the details as he might have at a party or in the street. He saw that the eyes were blacker than paint, were shiny – they moved and glared, refused to settle and were caught with a trembling nervousness which did not show in his hands or fingers.

He wore an anorak which was badly crumpled as if slept in overnight, and his jeans were dirty. Kind wanted to say something, to have some basis for understanding what was happening and what might happen, but he did not dare. He felt anger rise briefly and then die as his wife's fingers twined endlessly in his, pressing for a comfort which was beyond him. He did not know what to say, felt distanced from all this. He had been *writing*. Had been expecting mid-morning coffee soon and a small chat about Daniel, about how the last page had gone. There was a shotgun now pointing at him, at his wife and child – a shotgun which might tear open flesh, might kill them.

The room's silence was broken by the sound of Daniel's voice. "Mummy."

Jo, now taking both hands for her son, said, "Ssh. Ssh my love."

Mercifully, it seemed enough for Daniel, who turned again to stare at the man with the shotgun, whose eyes moved on as if watching for sudden movement elsewhere in the lounge.

Kind found himself listening carefully to the sounds the other men made. He heard drawers being opened upstairs and in the kitchen someone picked up the wall telephone and replaced it again after two or three seconds. No one said a word.

Kind thought: If they go near Daniel's window at the front the people opposite might see.

Yes, this was possible, was just possible. Kind held the thought to him like a comfort.

Downstairs of course, the possibility was less likely. The house was built with both main rooms – the kitchen and lounge – at the back where the view was of shrubs and a high stone wall. Apart from the small window on the stairs and the downstairs bathroom window (which was of dimpled glass anyway) there was no ground-floor view onto the street. The bedrooms were slightly more open but only marginally so and even the small, paved garden was protected by walls or high hedges.

A timid desperation seized Kind and he tried to shrug it away. He felt tense, realized that his stomach was tensed hard and when he tried to relax he found it almost impossible.

The leader came back in then, followed immediately by the man he had sent upstairs who just said quietly, almost in an embarrassed way, "Nothing there."

How could there be room for embarrassment? Kind was brushed by a feeling of the absurdity of what had happened.

The first man now nodded and turned to look at Kind. They stared at each other in silence for some moments and Kind wished that he could stand, felt awkward to be on the couch while these stangers paraded their guns and private conversations.

He took in more details.

The man he was facing was several years younger than himself. Shorter too, perhaps five feet nine, no more. His hair was black but in a cleaner, less oiled way than his companion's − it curled a little at the ends, giving a slightly boyish look, except that his mouth was loose, his lips parted and that belied the young expression somehow, impressed Kind with its sense of tired age. All these men looked tired.

He looked again, trying not to offend, not to challenge.

The pistol was held towards the floor as if the man was unaware of it or perhaps was simply unsurprised by the power it gave him. Now that the house had been declared safe he had a more casual, almost amused air as he studied Kind's face and appeared to make his own judgements.

What now?

The pause went on and on and then at last broke with movement.

The man walked over to the round lounge table, and drew out one of the hard wooden chairs ranged round it, dragging the chair over the carpet until it was immediately in front of Kind, back towards him. The man then straddled the chair in a faintly posing way, resting his hands on the chair-back and pointing his pistol at Kind's face.

Jesus Christ. Kind was so frightened he forced himself to speak first.

"Do you plan to harm us? My wife or child?"

"Not if they're good." The man's voice was milder now, slightly less brutal, but he seemed taken back by Kind's question, somehow caught off guard and now something in his face showed that he resented this.

Kind said nothing. He looked at the pistol and tried to imagine the pain of bullets, the shock of them. The vacuum he had felt, the absence of sharp emotion, was filling up and the overwhelming, hardening sensation was of personal terror. Kind knew that he must discover the intentions of these men, he could not allow them to hurt his family. He told himself this and swallowed and tried to put aside his own fear but it was painfully difficult.

Outside in the garden, a blackbird perched on the pergola poles and sang. It was a sweet, clear and surprising sound.

The man in front of him said, "I'm going to ask you some questions and I want you to answer straight away, no mucking about. Right?"

The pistol was still pointing at Kind's eyes. "Yes," he said. "OK."

The man's face was perhaps three feet from his, the pistol eighteen inches.

The man spoke again. "First, does anyone else live here?"

"No."

"Quite certain?"

Kind forced himself to nod. "Yes."

"Second, is anyone going to call today?"

Were they? Kind was silent for a while but just could not think clearly, so he turned to his wife and found her watching with a tension in her face which he found disturbing, saddening.

"Jo? Are we expecting anyone?"

"No." Her voice was deeper than usual, he noted; it sounded almost coarse.

The man with the pistol broke in again, "What about tonight? Or tomorrow?"

Tomorrow ... ? How long did they plan to stay?

Kind shook his head. Jo said, "No."

At this, the man with the gun sat back a little and appeared to relax still further. It seemed almost as though he had been frightened but, once committed, had discovered an ease he had not anticipated. Kind wondered if he dared risk a question yet, but decided to wait.

The sight of the guns was the only shocking thing about the scene; there was nothing else alarming, just three men – two of them standing, one sitting back a little waiting to find more words. Kind was surprised at how quickly the intrusion seemed normal, almost acceptable. And yet it was absurd that he should be held captive in his own lounge for no reason – or no reason that he knew.

Behind the seated intruder the other two men stood watchfully, nervously by the open door to the hall. The thin, wild-eyed young man with the shotgun was now pointing it at the floor, while his friend had put away his pistol somewhere and held his hands together in front in a terribly mild way.

Their leader now spoke again.

"I expect you're wondering who we are?"

Kind nodded. Said nothing.

The man went on. "Well as far as you're concerned

we're three naughty boys who want to stay here for a bit
while some things get sorted."

Kind still said nothing and this appeared to irritate the
man.

"All right?" he asked sharply.

"All right."

"Good. Right." The man looked over his shoulder at
his friend with the shotgun. "OK, Reg?"

The reply was a short, high grunting noise. It was a
curious sound and Kind automatically looked over in his
direction – a glance caught by the man in the chair who
said sharply, "Something you want?"

Kind shook his head quickly. "No," he said.

"Good. Well I'll tell you what *we* want." The man
nodded at Jo as he went on in an abrupt, harsh voice,
"We want your good lady here to go into the kitchen and
make us some food and bring it here." Looking back at
Kind he added, "And where's your booze?"

"It's only home-made." The apology sounded almost
cowardly; perhaps it was.

The man just said, "Piss."

Kind said nothing.

A silence fell and the two men stared at each other,
then the gunman half-shouted, "Well go on then! Get it.
Move yourself."

Almost in a jerking, frightened way, Kind leaned
forward to stand up, but realized in that second that he
would not be able to do so unless the other man moved
the chair back a little; he hesitated, hating himself for the
indecision, waiting for the move, and when it did not
come, looked up. He understood then exactly how the
other man was feeling – knew it at once. There was a
taunting look in the eyes, a kind of fascination. It was a
disturbing look and Kind felt afraid once more. He said
quietly, "Excuse me."

Still the man waited. He nodded a little, mouth

hanging open in that loose, tired way. Then at last, almost grudgingly, he slid the chair back over the carpet without bothering to stand or look over his shoulder. He watched Kind's eyes all the time and the expression of mocking interest did not change.

Hearing the chair legs scrape up the carpet pile, Kind winced. He stood up, feeling his heart beating far too quickly, then paused, looked quickly at Jo and said, "Love? Do you want to come and make some food?"

She stared up at him as if deaf or entranced. Said nothing and he was forced to repeat the question in a quieter, soothing way. Jo appeared to shake briefly and then she nodded and said, "Yes." Her voice, he noticed, remained deep and scared.

She stood, still holding onto Daniel who by now was beginning to wriggle and lose his shyness. Without looking at the men Jo asked, "What do you want?"

"Food." The leader's reply was condescending, sarcastic.

"But what – "

"It's all right, love," Kind broke in. "We'll settle that outside, shall we?"

He took her arm and led her towards the door. She walked like a child, a frightened child. The seated man called, "Go with them Reg. Harry-boy and I have some business to discuss."

The two men standing between Kind and the door moved a little to one side to let him pass and he ushered Jo out with great care, sensing rather than seeing, the man called Reg follow them out into the hall and through into the kitchen.

There was just a chance, Kind thought, that someone in the road might glance in now and glimpse the shotgun through the stairs window (and call the police and bring *help*, for God's sake). He even walked slowly in order to increase the chances of this happening, but was pushed slightly from behind and dared not risk further delay.

In the kitchen, which was quite small and full of early summer sunlight, he turned to Jo and told her to make sandwiches.

"Cheese and pickle, that sort of thing," he added, feeling pathetic, feeling ludicrous.

"But ... " Jo seemed lost. She blinked several times, hugged Daniel close and seemed about to cry. To their side the man with the shotgun stood in the doorway, thin and dirty, watching them without a word. He was only three or four feet away from them and his shotgun was held at hip height like a pike or spear. Kind tried to imagine grabbing the gun, wrenching it free from the man's hands and turning it on him – but he could not do so. It seemed improbable. Fantastic.

Very quietly, Jo went on again in a questioning, childish tone. "Are we just going to feed them?"

She seemed stunned by what had happened – even more so than Kind himself who had been subtly prepared for the shock by the sound of Jo's voice calling up the stairs and by the instinct which had made him conceal the paper-knife. He wanted to ask her what had happened, how they had come in and what they had said – but again, did not dare risk it.

"We'll do as they say, love," he said gently. "Put Daniel on the chair and make the sandwiches. Please."

He was coaxing her, trying to be calm, but Jo still hesitated, pulled her son closer for one moment as if suddenly afraid for him.

"Come on," insisted Kind. "Put him down. He'll be all right with us."

Reluctantly, Jo at last eased her grip on the boy, turned and placed him on a chair at the kitchen table, where he wriggled at once and tried to get down.

Kind called sharply, "No! Stay there!"

And instantly there came a shout from the lounge,

"Reg?"

At the door, the man with the shotgun made two sounds – nothing like words, just two quick monotones – and Kind realized that the man was mute. He had suspected it a few minutes before in the lounge but now it was confirmed and he stared with intense curiosity which was greeted by slight, jerking movements of the shotgun.

Quite slowly, turning away to the kitchen cupboard by the back door, the possible significance of this new fact came to Kind together with a more powerful feeling of fear. He opened the cupboard door and busied himself among the bottles which were cluttered together in semi-darkness on the shelves at the back. There was wine and beer. He hesitated and then took two bottles of wine and placed them carefully on the table where Daniel at once reached out for them with eager, playful fingers. Then he bent back into the cupboard and took out four bottles of beer and then four more. Then he began taking out some glasses and a tray, all the while examining the frightening thought which had occurred to him with the sound of those two inarticulate noises.

Of all distinguishing marks, Kind realized, the inability to speak must be among the most distinctive and rare. If this was the case and if the men who had invaded his home had made no attempt to conceal this fact (or hide their faces; they'd even used their own Christian names) then either they were complete fools or they knew that the information would be of no use to the captured family.

Kind put this thought to himself again and again, opening bottles, arranging glasses with far too much care on the tray with a hunting scene on it.

And this meant?

Now gathering up the bottle-tops. Putting them into the bin under the sink.

This meant that there was a new threat to his wife and child, to himself. He discussed it silently with himself and could only confirm it, repeat it and again and again like a silent warning. He almost wanted to cry, wanted to say, Stop, it's a game, a silly game ...

He tried to be brave but found that it was only possible to *act* bravely, not to feel that way; and so he worked steadily and carefully but felt almost painfully scared.

For a moment, he regretted not having fought the men from the first, to get it over with. But then he dismissed this as irrational, emotional – like much of his writing, the words which ended up on that vicious spike upstairs.

No. Kind understood that resistance in such a blind way would have been foolish and hopelessly inadequate. There were three men, all of them armed, and though their purpose was unclear it seemed that, for the moment at least, it was in their interests not to harm Kind or his family – perhaps for reasons of security, or a need for hostages. Kind did not know, could only guess endlessly. Yet it did seem clear that, even without immediate danger, something must change shortly, must be done to prevent this appalling scene from continuing as he feared.

The choices.

Kind took pickle from the cupboard and gave it to Jo. She looked surprised. Her round and pretty face seemed genuinely shocked at this piece of thoughtfulness, as if it had no place at this time. Kind smiled but his wife just stared for a while and then looked away as if not understanding. He knew he ought to feel very close to her but did not, not at this moment.

The choices were dreadfully simple.

They could wait and hope that the men would leave them alone, would go away eventually when whatever they were waiting for happened or arrived. Also hope that the men would not care about identification, would not mind leaving them in peace when it was over. This was a possibility.

Or?

Kind closed his eyes for one second, struggling to think logically at a time when he felt overwhelmed by emotion. The second possibility, the second choice ...

To identify some method of telling people outside what had happened – and to do that without panicking these men, perhaps forcing them to violence. Kind suspected – no, *knew* – that they would be capable of panic.

Or?

To decide which form of attack might best succeed. This was the most frightening, most reluctant consideration and yet somehow it also seemed the most plausible, God knew why. Success would depend, he imagined, solely upon how many of the men remained in one room at any time, how many stayed in the house. There ought to be a formula, a cold statement of facts for which he must watch, must be prepared to use.

Kind, glancing again at Jo, watching Daniel play with the bottle-opener on the cold, white kitchen table, felt lonely. The paper-knife hidden under his shirt at the back of his jeans was digging in and hurting a little. A mocking pain.

He picked up the tray to take it back into the other room and at the door said, "Excuse me." His voice shook a little and he hoped that Jo would not notice – she had always seemed anxious that he should face things, always wanted to fan the fire in him, had laughed at his life-insurance patter, had praised him for America. What would *she* expect now?

The man with the shotgun backed away slowly and the muzzle of the weapon followed Kind as he turned left and walked into the lounge.

Four

The men who had made prisoners of Kind and his family in such a bizarre way were more dangerous than he could have known, but the reasons for this would also have surprised him.

On the face of it they seemed experienced, possibly vicious criminals, used to handling weapons and working together outside the law. This was not so. None of the three men in the house that morning had more than minor criminal records and only one of them – the leader, the man with the wide, thick lips – had ever fired a weapon of any kind: he had once been in the Territorial Army and had used an old Lee Enfield .303 rifle on military ranges.

What made them dangerous was not their familiarity with crime but the reverse of that: their fear of it, their uncertainty. The decision to stop at Kind's house and take prisoners had been made only a few seconds before it actually happened. It was a badly considered move and amateurishly executed (their car was still parked fifty yards from the house on the main road; their weapons had been clumsily concealed in their coats when they knocked at the door and Jo Kind answered). The possibility therefore – sensed by Kind but not properly understood – was that whatever else they did would be equally spontaneous and stupid. They were reacting from moment to moment in an atmosphere of extreme tension which they themselves had created.

The leader of the small group was a man called Gregory Atkins, always called Greg except when on official forms. He was 25 years old and still lived with his

parents in a block of council flats in Southwark, South
London. He worked one day a week selling vegetables on
a market stall, for which he was paid in cash. This,
together with unemployment benefit, enabled him to get
through week by week without having to take a full-time
job, and this was important to him – he would ask
acquaintances or his few friends the single, mocking
question: "What's the fucking point?" Mostly he would
laugh then – a thin, nasal sound always tinged by
sarcasm, whatever the joke.

Atkins had lived this way since leaving school at the age
of 15. His short experience with the TA had been nothing
more than a swiftly soured dream from which he had
awoken sharply after a parade-ground row with an
officer-greengrocer. Atkins rarely made facts of his
dreams; mostly drifted with them.

His parents would have objected to his life-style but
they were quite old and he was their only child – also,
they were a little afraid of him: not that their son was
particularly violent, only that it seemed at times that he
could be, might be if he dared. His open-mouthed
silences would disturb them in a way they could not
explain properly to each other. If they asked questions
which he did not want to answer he would stare until they
looked away; then he would say, "All right?" or
something mocking which would leave them feeling
uneasy and somehow threatened. If he was drunk Atkins
would turn off the television and talk and his parents
would listen and listen, not offering anything more than
agreement even when he spoke of crimes he might one
day commit, robberies which were just ripe (they were
always ripe). Atkins would go on like this quite often. It
was a theme with him and again his parents never
questioned it, or believed him.

In the days between queuing at the benefit office and
selling vegetables, Atkins spent his time in a series of cafés

and amusement arcades in South London where the company was instant and transitory. Groups would form, merge, spread and redefine themselves and the constant flow gave him the sense of purpose he really needed – the idea of movement and progress which his old schoolfriends (now rarely seen) supposedly derived from slaving forty hours a week in factories: "Stupid bastards. Stupid arse-licking bastards."

Atkins was good with fruit machines and had a small local reputation for this: the wave of electronic games had absorbed him for months until he worked out the programmes which seemed common to them all and then fell back on the older, standard machines he had grown up with. He spent a lot of money this way but sometimes made a little too, using this as an excuse to get drunk, mostly during the day – he liked drinking by daylight, seldom did it by night. After such a session, he would go home, turn off the sport and start telling his father about some of the ideas he had, some of the schemes they had discussed down at the pub. His father, of course, neither understood nor cared, and his placid, nodding responses often made Atkins angry ...

Atkins drew most of his friends from the series of half-familiar faces which filled his arcade days, relying on none of them and offering each only a brittle, sarcastic humour for amusement; mostly, these friends would come and go and never bothered discussing anything ("Anything *real*," Atkins would complain) unless drunk.

When they did talk it was schemes again, ideas on the fringe of the law or well over it, which might make a fortune. Second-hand cars was one. "Wind the clocks back, shift them out of town. Deal in cash." Furniture was another. Door-knocking in country areas for the flash stuff they sold in the quiet, pricey shops across town which always made Atkins feel somehow unclean and resentful. This scheme, like the cars and all the others,

came to nothing more than beer-talk, but what linked it
to the general drift of his ideas was the belief that country
areas were rich for picking, were ripe for plunder. Atkins,
in fact, seldom left Southwark. He rarely had cause to,
but he remained convinced that things could not be so
tough where grass and trees grew and that, consequently,
the people there would be more naïve, less resilient than
the groups and gangs of familiar faces in the arcades and
cafes. No contest. A walk-over in any confrontation.
These people could be used, he felt, somehow they could
be used.

Amongst all his transient friends, only one could claim
anything like real loyalty or even affection. This was the
burning-eyed, thin-faced young man with the shotgun.
The mute. His name was Reg Daley and he lived two
streets away from Atkins in another Southwark council
block. Theirs was an odd relationship which no one really
understood – Atkins was quite clever in an evasive way,
but Daley was not only unable to speak, he was
emotionally unstable and quite possibly retarded. Yet the
two men spent a lot of time together and seemed to enjoy
each other in some way, to be reassured by the other's
presence in all that shifting, re-forming flow of people. It
was strange. Atkins would give orders to the mute in a
careless, mocking fashion: small orders, unimportant
details – fetching cigarettes, changing money for the
machines. The mute would obey without one sign of
resentment. People did not know why and inevitably
made the odd sexual joke, though, again, never to
Atkins's face.

The two young men had been friends for some years
and it was inevitable that when Atkins finally decided to
break the law in a significant way he should take Daley
with him.

This happened almost entirely by mistake.

Among the drunken dreams which Atkins considered

in daylight pubs was one treasure to which he returned time and time again. It was inspired largely by newspaper stories of criminals who used the motorway system to carry out jobs miles from their home town. This seemed a clever, exciting prospect to Atkins and somehow less dangerous than robbing places you knew, real places with everyday problems like police, alarms, neighbours and so on – these things mattered less at a distance. Crime was easier to imagine like this.

The importance of crime to Atkins was not simply the money. He talked of crime, dreamed of it, as a kind of social regulator, a fair balance, something which repaid the people in pricey shops for the sense of unease they inspired in him. Crime was right. Greed glamorized by justice, the kind of back-bar justice which came in forcefully with the third pint and yet lingered through all the drifting days. Atkins resented poverty almost as much as he resented those who were not poor. And it would not have mattered, would never have been important what he felt or thought, had it not been for one key meeting which pushed the dream into reality; also for the misunderstanding.

It began over a pin-ball machine in a dirty, loud and open-fronted amusement arcade right on the fringes of Southwark – a place which marked the furthest border to which Atkins was normally prepared to travel for his pleasures. Luckily, the arcade was on a decent bus route so he went there quite often though rarely further, or not for slot machines anyway.

The meeting happened at about eleven o'clock one morning mid-week and was a matter of chance. Atkins was alone because Reg Daley was spending the morning on a fill-in job humping coal. Not all the eyes bothered to move as he walked into the place but most of the bowed heads nodded to him as he took his place at a vacant machine and slipped in a coin.

After a few minutes' play a plump young man who seemed out of place in a tweed jacket strolled up and began to watch. He saw the way Atkins played and said, "Good," quietly, flatteringly. Atkins played on, watching the numbers rise, comforted by the flashing lights and sudden ring of bells.

When a difficult ball slipped by the metal flippers, causing Atkins to writhe in brief, hopeless anguish, the man at his elbow said, "I thought you had that."

Atkins said, "Bastard machine."

They both laughed.

It was the last ball and he switched from that game to another, falling into conversation with the plump young man as naturally as he had done with others on other occasions – pausing, breathless conversations in between shots and pulls.

They parted after a while to play separately but then returned to adjoining machines and fed in coins. Atkins won a ten-pound jackpot. The noise of it brought up all the faces, all the expressions of envy; hammer-blows as the machine thudded out coin after coin.

"Done it!" said the stranger. "You jammy old sod."

One or two bystanders who knew Atkins waited for him to get angry at this but for some reason he did not. In fact, on scooping up his pile of coins and marching off for a drink, Atkins paused to call the stranger after him and that was how they met, how the project began and the mistake was made.

Five

The leader, the man Greg Atkins, was talking quietly and secretively to the third member of the group when Kind walked in with the tray and put it carefully on the dining-table. He hesitated, torn ludicrously by a host-urge to open the bottles and pour out the beer and wine for his captors, aware that this was an inappropriate, almost cowardly thing to consider. In the end he said, "There's beer or wine," and stood there waiting.

The leader pointed to the couch again and said, "Sit down, you."

As Kind did so, both men took a bottle each and, in silence, eased open the tops and began pouring. Both misjudged the froth and spilt a little on the carpet. Atkins then laid his pistol on the table in order to pour and take a first, deep and thirsty gulp of beer. Immediately he had done so he picked up the gun and took glass and pistol over to the corner chair, into which he sprawled carelessly.

Kind, risking the moment at last, asked quietly, "Are you going to tell me what you want with us?"

There was a pause.

Atkins appeared to consider the question, his lips hanging open, eyes staring at the spot on the carpet where the froth had spilt. Kind recognized the mocking insult of the performance and again was disturbed by it; even the man's silence seemed an exercise of unaccustomed power. He was enjoying himself, using the scene for some private purpose. The atmosphere was tense once more. The other man, Kind sensed, seemed to be just as much on edge as he felt.

At last, as if giving a weighty judgement, Atkins answered, "What we want out of you is co-operation." He paused. Sipped beer and went on, "If we get it I might decide to be nice for a change. If we don't – and I mean this – you'll regret the day you was ever born. And your wife. And your nice little boy."

Kind hated him. Wanted to laugh for all this cliché talk, but replied carefully, "Do you plan to stay here?"

"For a while."

"May I ask why?"

Something about the question, or perhaps the way he asked it, caused the other man's brief good humour to break. He half-shouted, "No you fucking may not! You keep your mouth shut until I speak to you and don't ask questions – see?"

Kind nodded, said nothing.

The man watched him for some seconds in complete silence before going on suddenly, "When I want to tell you something I will. We'll be here for a bit yet and when we go … " His voice trailed off briefly and he seemed to struggle with inner thoughts as if facing a new problem. Then he said, "I'll fucking let you know. All right?"

Again, Kind nodded but kept quite silent. He recognized signs of danger in the man's sudden outburst and felt his heartbeat quicken in response. The man did not seem to know what would happen when they left – this was what frightened Kind, made him feel sweat in his hands and down his back.

The gunman continued to stare at him for a while, open-mouthed and challenging as if waiting for the slightest excuse for more anger. When it did not come he returned to his beer in an almost sulking way, gulping some down and then saying, "Piss," to his friend, who laughed quietly and fell silent. It seemed that this man too was waiting for Atkins to make the running, to give all the signals. Kind looked at the third member of the group and tried to judge him but found it difficult.

Somehow, he seemed unlike his friends. He was young, perhaps 20 or maybe even less, Kind was not sure. The few words he had heard him utter had indicated a middle-class education and background (the leader sounded as rough as he acted) and the lines of his face seemed pleasant, almost polite. He was quite slim and rather short; his clothes seemed more fashionable than practical and this was another surprise: tight trousers, dashes of colour to mark him out and draw attention – bright red belt, green flecks on the collar of his shirt ...

Kind, watching the man in small, risked glances from his seat on the couch, realized with a kind of guilty shock that what really separated him from the other two was something like class. It seemed a shaming thought at such an intensely practical moment; lives were in danger and Kind was sensing a kinship which mocked his own egalitarian principles. Perhaps not shaming, just funny, but Kind lacked the humour for it just then, only felt bitter.

He wondered then what, if anything, any of this meant and for the next few seconds was captured by new feelings of fear from which he only escaped with effort. Thinking about the future – the next moment and the next – hurt him now.

The silence in the room had become oppressive.

From next door came small, irritating sounds of sandwich-making but nothing else and Kind thought: Daniel's being good.

Exactly then, eerily as if in answer to Kind's fear, there came a small thump from the kitchen and the swift, childish pad of feet followed by a brief cry from Jo. She was too late. The boy slipped past the shotgun guard and appeared suddenly in the lounge, grinning as if aware that he had been naughty. Kind, caught as always by the sudden beauty of his son – the clouded haze of white hair, the pouting, luscious red mouth which seemed so absurdly sensual – called softly, "Go back to Mummy, love. Go on. Go and see Mummy."

There were noises at the kitchen door.

As Daniel stood undecided, still hoping for a game, Jo's voice came sharply, almost hysterically, "Let me – out!" There was a sudden cry and sounds of a struggle which made Kind jump up in a mixture of anger and fear.

"Stay there."

The order came, inevitably, from the leader, who was slower in rising.

Kind ignored him and began half-running towards the kitchen, even pushing to one side the third young man, who seemed suddenly alarmed.

"Stop!"

This time, the voice held a threat which caused Kind to stop at once, caught just by the open door.

Slowly, he turned to find that the pistol was pointing directly at his head and that the eyes beyond were alive with panic.

"All right," said Kind. "All right, all right."

Jo began crying in the kitchen – a slow, low sound which caused Daniel to turn and run out of the lounge, the only moving thing in the room. The three men stood quite still, each held by the same dangerous trance which showed clearest in Atkins's fierce, almost lunatic eyes. Staring back at him, Kind understood that he had almost been shot. Also, that in another moment, this might still happen. There was no comparison in his life for this second, no equal. He felt faint; the unreality seized him again and he repeated, "All right."

The words seemed to trigger a new stage of madness. Atkins blinked and lowered the pistol from arm's length to his hip, removing as he did so only a little of the menace of his pose. Slowly he walked forward until he was a foot away from Kind, and at this distance the difference in their height was more striking. It seemed to make the man even more angry. His thick lips were pulled back in an unhealthy, gasping way and his teeth showed yellowish beneath. Carefully, almost experimentally, he brought up the pistol, took it right over his own shoulder and brought down the butt on Kind's forehead.

Kind tried not to flinch. He was aware of a soft cracking noise and a sharp but not blinding pain. And then silence.

Opening his eyes from their instinctive wince, Kind stared at his attacker, who stood with his hand still raised as if considering another blow. The first had not really been successful – Kind had neither fallen to the ground nor cried out. It had been an inexpert blow, a test which had gone wrong. Staring straight into those speculative, angry eyes, Kind realized that the man had never done such a thing before, that he was even now re-examining the moment, savouring its effect like a first taste of blood.

As calmly as he could, Kind said, "That was unnecessary."

"I warned you to stop." The reply was surprisingly mild, even defensive.

Kind said, "He's hurting my wife in there."

"If you do that again I'll shoot you."

"Then everyone would hear."

Kind knew he should not challenge the man but could not stop himself – felt almost proud that he had enough courage to be so silly. He looked down on the gunman and hated him; hated the pain which still throbbed in his forehead; hated the restraint of being unable to run in and help Jo simply because this person told him not to. He felt the third man watching but did not dare turn to see.

As if answering the emotion in Kind's face, Atkins reacted in an inevitable and frighteningly slow fashion.

He brought down the pistol from over his shoulder and moved his wrist and arm until the muzzle was touching Kind's cheek. Then he reached up with his other hand and pulled back the hammer until it fixed with a small click. Then he paused.

Kind felt almost literally petrified by fear. The touch of the barrel just below his left eye was electric, cold and furious; alive. The sound of the hammer cocking was intimate and evil; a suckling sound, a prelude. The silent pause which followed was filled with noise from his heart.

Kind realized that he was trembling. Believed that this man longed to shoot him, as he had wanted to hit, to taste more power, more blood. He dared say nothing. Could only wait, knowing that his life now depended upon a single sliver of metal which kept the hammer of the pistol from falling onto the explosive cap of the bullet, also upon that thread of moral recognition which was just visible behind the eyes of the armed man: perhaps, only perhaps, this person was not yet ready to kill.

At this moment, something else moved in the room. It was the third man, the silent one who had seemed prepared to watch and agree with his friend only seconds before. Now he took two paces forward so that he was standing close to the two men and, facing his friend, said, "We've got some things to check up on, Greg."

Even in his fear, Kind could recognize the shake in his voice, hear its sudden timidity. The politeness was there too – at such a moment. How funny.

The man said again, "Greg?"

This time it worked. Atkins sniffed, a jerking, violent sound as if shaking himself free of some hold. He lowered the pistol in a brusque way and carelessly used both hands to lower the hammer, stepping back and looking away from Kind as if embarrassed, or as if there never had been a threat at all. Kind knew that this was a lie; that he had almost died just then. He also understood that the man called Greg (the first time he had heard him named) had stepped back from killing only because it was a new experience and he was taking these things carefully. Perhaps next time he would complete the scene; or perhaps it would be later. Kind wanted to thank the other man for his help but knew that this would be an impossible gesture.

As if suddenly tired of the gun, Atkins thrust it into his belt just in front of the hip – almost cowboy-fashion – and brushed past Kind without bothering to look at him.

In the instant that was available to him, Kind considered turning on the one who remained. His pistol was nowhere to be seen, presumably in the man's pocket. He was small, slight. Kind almost moved to attack him – but within the space of that instant realized that this was not the correct formula he had been seeking: to disarm one man while the other two were alone with his wife and child would be pointless, an action which could only end in appalling failure. He did nothing, only asked in a whisper, "What is it you want?"

The young man looked at him, hesitated and then under cover of voices starting up in the kitchen, whispered back, "Nothing. We're just waiting to speak to someone. We'll go soon."

Kind did not believe him, did not believe that this man had the power to make that sort of promise. He turned and walked out, aware that even if the man had threatened him with a gun he would still have done so: he was so different from the one they called Greg.

In the kitchen he found Jo sitting at the table hugging Daniel, looking away from the two men who stood above her. As Kind waited in the doorway, watching, Atkins was saying, "You didn't ought to upset him, love. You ought to be a bit careful around Reg."

Jo said nothing. Her head was bowed and she was clinging to Daniel as if trying to lose herself in him, to escape through the soft warmth of his body.

Slowly, again as if trying out the movement to see how it felt, Atkins raised his left hand and touched her hair. He kept it there for a moment as if fascinated and Kind stepped forward saying, "Stop that – "

Reg, the mute, half turned towards him and raised the shotgun until it pointed at his stomach. Atkins looked up and watched Kind come to a halt; he smiled and continued to stroke Jo's hair as if, now tried, he liked the feel of it.

Her hair was soft and shining black. Quite short. His
hand followed the gentle curve of it again and again, each
time touching the nape of her neck and she did not move
and neither did Kind. Both could only suffer the
experience; feel it, burn with it.

Six

Kind, sitting now at the kitchen table holding his wife's
hand, was grateful for her silence because it allowed him
to think.

The mute stood at the door, on guard with precisely
the vigilance his friend had askesd for, shotgun pointing
at the table only a degree or so from Kind's chest. His
dark, glinting eyes continued to flicker over the room,
appearing never to settle on one point for longer than a
moment. After the row about Daniel he seemed even
more nervous than before, as if his pride had been stung
or he had been shamed in some way.

Daniel himself was now thoroughly upset. He wanted
to get down and go out into the garden where the mild
sun looked enchanting through the kitchen window, but
every time he struggled to get out his mother clung on
tightly until he gave up and relaxed. He was just a short
step away from tears and Kind, elbows on the white
plastic table top, watched him and waited for the
outburst.

He tried to understand the situation, to find possible
explanations.

The timid young man had said that they were waiting
to speak to someone – but to whom? and for what
purpose? And above all the question remained over what
happened when they had found the man they wanted, had

spoken.

Kind tried again to estimate the chances of seeking outside help. These were remote, and it was his own fault. Since giving up work he and Jo had withdrawn into themselves a little, impressing on their friends the need for long, undisturbed silences. Kind had felt rather pretentious making this stipulation because at the time he had had little confidence in his own ability to write; telling others not to disturb him had seemed pathetic. Yet it had worked. People believed him and stayed away. Today was Wednesday – they expected no friends to call until Saturday at the earliest when normally they might have drinks at lunch-time with a couple who lived ten miles away.

They knew people in the street outside, but only to pass and nod to – simply for weather-chat and garden comments. No one, glimpsing men through the stairs window, would wonder at the presence of three stangers in the house (unless they saw the guns; a possibility).

Tradesmen? Kind let go of Jo's hand and wished he could check this point with her because she knew more about it than he did. Yet he did not dare ask her, not even casually in a guarded way, because she was obviously too upset to reply discreetly – a fact which disturbed and surprised him, made him sad but left him room to wonder at this new corner of his wife's character only just uncovered; he had not expected this breakdown.

It was a strange thing. On holiday in Devon just two months ago, Daniel had uncovered an adder which had reared up as if to strike. In fact the creature was too far away from the boy to be a great danger but Jo either did not see this or did not care: she stepped forward and swung her raffia picnic basket at the snake again and again while shrieking at her husband to get the boy away. Kind had done so and then killed the adder with a flat stone. Jo was later sick because she hated snakes.

It was odd that she should collapse so completely when faced with this human threat.

In as detailed a form as possible, Kind went over in his mind the list of tradesmen who might be expected to call.

Postman? Had been once already and as it was now eleven-thirty a second delivery seemed unlikely. Anyway, they would have no cause to open the door to him unless he had a parcel to deliver, which was rare.

Milkman then. He collected money mid-morning on Thursday, tomorrow, but until then would have no reason to call.

Who else?

The possibilities were so few. Sometimes the secretary of the constituency Labour Party called without warning to discuss letters they planned to send to the weekly newspaper. It was a habit Kind had tried to discourage but the man was insensitive and had yet to understand that Kind had other work to do during the day. It was just possible that he might drop round. Also, it occasionally happened that the woman who lived across the road (Kind still did not know her name though she had lived there for two years) asked Jo to look after her baby while she went shopping – but again, Kind had been frowning on this lately because of the noise and so it might not happen again. Beyond that, very, very occasionally, they were canvassed by salesmen offering cut-price double-glazing or wall insulation.

Reviewing these possibilities, Kind considered how isolated the list made him feel. Whole hours, even days, might be taken out of his life before anyone would know. He was a vital part of nothing; allowed only a very little to concern him. Perhaps this explained the sentiment in his writing – the distance from people which ruined perspective.

Kind frowned. Daniel caught the gesture and tried to copy it. Kind smiled and so did the child and Jo, sensing the distraction, pulled Daniel closer. The look on the boy's face was now irritated and Kind said, "I shouldn't hold him quite so tightly, love."

His wife said nothing, did not respond in any way.

Kind returned to the problem of warning people outside about what was happening to his family.

If anyone did call, what would he do? Even if he or Jo were allowed to answer the door the men would be watching and listening, holding their pistols or shotgun on whoever remained as hostage. The slightest hint of betrayal could cause these men to become hysterical and Kind was by now convinced that the man called Greg might welcome an opportunity to become violent; might delight in it.

Therefore whatever method Kind used to warn a caller would have to be completely silent, quite undetectable. A written message seemed the only possibility – and this of course meant acquiring a pencil and some paper and then stealing time in which to write a note and conceal it. Then, how to deliver it? Kind considered the problem and decided that it might be best to shake hands with whoever called, hoping that the palmed message would be accepted without comment. This seemed so unlikely that he became angry with himself and discarded the idea with contempt.

The telephone?

Ironically, this was fixed to the wall just two feet above Kind's head. It seemed to tease, to taunt. With three dialled numbers he would be able to alert the police – he had once called the emergency operator when Jo went into labour and their car refused to start. He knew that the operator would take perhaps five seconds to answer and would then ask which service he wanted and, quite possibly, what his telephone number was: then there would be a contact delay and the problem of informing the police in as few words as possible that three armed men were holding his family hostage. What words to use? Kind tried several to himself and decided that the shortest, most effective sentence would be: I live at 4 Queen's Road, Haywards Heath. Armed men are holding me.

Kind estimated that the whole procedure from start to finish would require thirty seconds of privacy. It seemed impossible. Anyone sitting in the lounge would hear him dialling in the kitchen – he had heard the phone being lifted himself just minutes ago. The only place where the men might stand and *not* hear would be Kind's bedroom upstairs; the others were too near. What on earth would concentrate all three men in that room? A disturbance perhaps. Unlikely though. Almost impossible.

Kind put away the thought and concentrated on other methods of warning.

A fire? (Remembering films, bad stories he had read). No. It would be a long and uncertain process and would be almost certain to alert their captors before anyone outside noticed.

Kind felt an overwhelming sense of frustration. He was in danger, a captive just yards from safety. Yet he could think of nothing, no safe way to convey a warning even to a man standing in front of him asking for milk money.

The possibilities which remained, of course, were that he could wait until the men decided to go, risking that they would leave his family unharmed even though they would be in a position to later identify the gang; or he could attempt to disarm them himself. Returning to this last prospect once more, Kind now viewed it with almost as much disbelief as he considered his chances of telephoning out a warning. The blow on his forehead had been a sharp reminder of the reality of violence. Could he turn that reality? It seemed unlikely.

Carefully though, Kind tried once again to decide which formula would best allow him to attack the men, and after only a short time he arrived at a possible outline: one man at least must be out of the house; also, the two remaining men must be in separate rooms. Any other combination would almost certainly lead to one or all of Kind's family being hurt or killed. Therefore an attack under any other circumstances would be impossible. One man must leave the house, the others must be separated.

Kind believed that he might work towards this, but not until he knew what the men wanted and how long they planned to stay. This meant gleaning information from the three men. How?

Daniel said, "Daddy. Want wee."

Before he could answer, Jo said sharply, "I'll do it."

One of them always had to help Daniel in the toilet. Kind would have preferred to have taken the boy to the bathroom himself because that at least might have given him a few moments alone. Yet Jo's voice was too brittle; he could risk no argument. Instead, Kind turned to the mute and said, "Can my wife take the boy to the bathroom?"

The man half-cocked his head as if in query, and Kind repeated, "He wants to go to the bathroom. The toilet."

The man seemed to hesitate, dark eyes flitting between Kind and the little boy as if looking for evidence of a trick; he seemed worried. At last, without moving or looking away he opened his mouth and uttered a sharp, imperative noise.

Atkins answered at once from the lounge with a shout, "What's up, Reg?"

Reg simply grunted again and after a few moments Atkins appeared in the doorway looking suspiciously at Kind and his wife.

"What is it?" he asked.

"My boy would like to go to the toilet."

"Oh?"

"My wife could take him."

Atkins put his head on one side and appeared to adopt a theatrically thinking pose. This went on in silence for a few seconds until Jo interrupted to say quickly, "He needs to go."

It was a mistake; Kind recognized that at once.

The man's face changed sharply so that the look of challenging intimidation returned to his eyes. He said, "He can please himself then. You're not going anywhere, lady."

It was a brutal, unnecessary rebuff. Kind, knowing that he was being foolish, tried to argue. "He's only a child," he said quietly. "He does need to be looked after."

The result was another threatening silence in which the two men at the door glared in at him with a frightening and unquestionable hostility: the man with the shotgun seemed to take all guidance from his leader, even to the point of emotional direction. It seemed a disturbing, formidable alliance. Kind felt in awe of them at that moment.

When at last he spoke, Atkins was almost dismissively brief. He said, "If one of you moves from that table, Reg will use the gun. All right?"

Then he turned and vanished from sight. Kind heard him walk back into the lounge and begin talking to his other friend. Reg, unmoving, kept the shotgun pointing at the kitchen table.

Jo said, "Richard?" Her voice was begging, almost demanding. He shrugged. He could not look at her.

In a little while Daniel said again, more urgently, "Want wee. Mummy. Want wee."

Jo said, almost desperately, "Richard?"

He glanced at her, seemed to find an accusation in her eyes and looked away again. Daniel called out again and Jo said nothing, only looked at her husband as if in dis belief. She suddenly moved and even as Kind stretched out his hand to stop her he saw the shotgun moving in the doorway.

"Don't," he told Jo. "Don't stand up or he'll shoot Danny. Stay where you are."

He had hold of her arm and was pulling firmly, would have hurt her if necessary, would have done anything to prevent her from standing because he believed that the man at the door would be foolish enough to obey the order to shoot. Kind was very frightened. He pulled harder and felt Jo relax. She looked at him but said nothing.

After a short while they heard the sound of urine falling as Daniel wet his trousers and the liquid seeped onto Jo's skirt and then trickled onto the floor. Daniel began to cry and then so did Jo. The mute at the door made a small noise and from next door Atkins shouted, "Has he pissed himself yet?"

Kind was almost unable to control his anger but in a while he did. The urine smelt bitter, acid. His son was unconsolable in his tears. Next door, Atkins was talking quietly, sounded quite relaxed now. Kind decided that if he was to find out what the men planned to do it must be from this man, their leader, whom he knew only as Greg. Of the others, one appeared too frightened to speak, the other stood in the doorway holding a shotgun unable to utter a word.

Seven

The misunderstanding which led eventually to the seizure of Kind and his family was that the plump stranger Atkins met over the pin-ball machine believed that his new friend was an experienced criminal.

This was the impression Atkins deliberately gave for his own, usual reasons after drinking five pints of Guinness in a pub not far from the arcade.

"Some of the characters you get in here," he said quietly, secretively, "are right villians. There's at least one plain-clothes filth in here right now that *I* know about ... "

His new friend, now alone with him at a side-table, seemed impressed and encouraged further talk like this. Atkins made up hinted tangles with the law, saying that it was his policy now "never to get banged up in London again".

Atkins normally lied only through necessity but the newcomer seemed to touch an odd vanity in him and after a while he disclosed that he had spent two years in jail and was wanted for more than had ever been proved. In fact, Atkins had committed only juvenile crimes and had never been held in custody for longer than two or three hours: his adult law-breaking had been confined to minor acts of fraud involving the benefit office, and a few undiscovered illegalities with old cars. Real crime had always seemed to him to be too practical a step, too real a possibility – like work, factory hours and the same bus home each night. He had shunned crime so far through disbelief rather than honesty.

Yet now, moving eventually from one pub to another with the stranger, Atkins gradually adopted villainous poses, returning yet again to the theme of driving out of London to commit crimes, of using speed and distance to get away with things which the local police ("local" – a word he applied only outside London) could never understand. "Piss," he said, "easy as piss."

The young man he was drinking with listened not so much with care as with enthusiasm, almost delight. He was about the same age as Atkins but more boyish, and pallidly round-faced. He wore an old anorak over the tweed sports jacket and his finger-nails were clean. He looked like a clerk – also, possibly a homosexual; Atkins thought about this once or twice during the drinking bout but decided to wait and see. Once he had hurt a homosexual quite badly in the underground walkway at the Elephant and Castle; he had quite enjoyed that in a hesitant, fearful way.

Fortunately, during the three and a half hours they spent stumbling from pub to pub there was no hint of a sexual advance and when at last they stood blinking in the mild spring sunshine on the steps of their last public bar, it seemed impossible that they should end the meeting there.

Surprisingly, because he had been a passive partner so far, the stranger took the lead and suggested they take some cans and find a seat somewhere. Atkins agreed, and after a lot of walking which sobered both of them a little they finished up sprawled on the grass at Camberwell Green where the professional drunks base themselves and look at newcomers with suspicion.

Atkins and his friend, who said his name was Davies, Peter Davies, were oblivious of these glances; they opened cans of Newcastle Brown and sipped and watched the sky and the traffic.

After a while, Davies made the suggestion for which he had been seeking the courage over the past two hours – ever since he had decided that Atkins was indeed a man of criminal experience.

In a light, pausing tone which matched his boyish looks, he said, "You know I don't live around here."

"No?" Atkins glanced at him as if this was a point of interest.

"No. I'm from Crawley. My family came from here. Some still do. Still are."

Atkins was feeling friendly. "Crawley's OK," he said, "Lots of my mates got friends round there."

"Mm." Davies was silent. Waited. And then continued, "I work at this place there."

"Oh yes?"

"Cash and carry."

"What's it like?"

"All right. Big. Does a lot of business."

Atkins sipped Newcastle Brown. He was becoming drunk again. He said, "I couldn't stand the hours. Not day after day like that. I've got a barrow myself. We take a fortune on a good day. Hundreds of quid."

"I'm talking about hundreds of thousands. Tens of thousands anyway."

Atkins still did not see. He waited for the subject to change, and when it did not, was surprised.

"Five check-outs," said Davies. "Thirty loading staff. That's the sort of business I'm talking about. Do you know what I mean?"

Atkins grunted.

Along the edge of the green two uniformed policemen were beginning to shake and hustle the drunks. Atkins watched them and became nervous. Sometimes the policemen used a boot to push and prod a drunk awake and even the worst of the sprawled men got up and cowered away when told.

Davies said, "I know exactly how the place could be robbed."

At first, Atkins barely heard him, was more concerned with the slow progress of the policemen as they moved along the margin of the grass, never pausing to argue only to issue orders which he was too far away to catch but could imagine. Atkins did not want trouble; he wanted to be left in peace to finish his cans, was thinking that perhaps they might go somewhere else ...

His companion's message finally got through to his drink-fuddled mind.

"What?" he asked slowly, almost in disbelief.

The other man coughed as if suddenly nervous. He sat up on one elbow and stared at Atkins, apparently unaware of the distant policemen.

"I said I know how the place could be robbed," he repeated. Speaking much quicker, he went on, "I know how to get in, where the alarms are, who'd be around at what time and when the best day would be. I know everything." He seemed excited, alive suddenly. His words were tumbled out as if he could not wait to deliver them, must hurry them at Atkins before they grew stale or he lost confidence.

Atkins raised himself to one elbow and looked at the man. Half-sitting like this he found that his head cleared a little and he was able to understand what was being offered. Yet he still found it difficult to believe.

"Are you planning– " he struggled for the word " – a job?"

The other man shrugged, suddenly enigmatic. "I'm just saying what *could* be done," he said. "If the right people got together."

Atkins laughed, but then looked again at Davies and stopped abruptly. "You serious?" he asked in a doubting voice.

Again, the man shrugged. He said nothing.

Atkins glanced over to the policeman and saw that at last one was looking his way. He licked his lips. He sat up properly and began arranging his empty and full cans into one group so that he could pick them all up at once if necessary.

The pause seemed to worry the other man who said, "I'm only saying what could be done. If someone wanted a lot of money, say. I'm not saying I would but I could though. I mean, I could tell someone what to do, someone who knew ... "

The policeman began walking over the grass towards them and Atkins stood up. Davies, unaware of the approach, began to get excited as if frightened of losing an opportunity which had been a long time coming.

"I could make it very easy," he gabbled, "I could show someone just which way to get in so no one would know. I could – "

"Shut it!"

Atkins's violent, whispered shout entirely broke the other man's stream of words.

His round, white face looked hurt. He stared up at Atkins in silence for a moment, noting the way he gathered up his cans in a hurried, nervous way.

The arrival of the policeman came as a complete shock – a sudden bulky intrusion of blue which sprang like a nightmare before his eyes. He became speechless. The policeman looked tired and fed up, but something about the rather formal clothes which Peter Davies was wearing made him adopt a more gentle approach than he might have chosen if Atkins had been alone. He said that they had been asked to clear the grass area for the moment and asked if they could take their drink elsewhere.

Atkins at once said, "Yes. Right-ho, mate. Come on – " He was about to call Peter Davies by name but something held him back. Davies, staring from Atkins to the policeman, did not move.

The policeman said, "Now come on, don't muck me about … "

His careful temper was thinning and in another few minutes he would have become angry. Atkins, seeing this, bent down and took his friend by the arm, pulling him to his feet, coaxing him with a false smile and anxiously cheerful words. "All right, mate, we'll go to your aunty's, come on. Get your booze now, come on … "

The desperation of his tone at last made itself clear to Davies, who began hurriedly collecting himself, gathering up his own cans, straightening his clothes – while the policeman stood silently watching.

The two made their way over the grass and out onto the pavement without speaking. They picked a road at

random and began walking, but after only a few minutes
Atkins glanced behind, turned to the stranger and
stopped him with a hand on the arm. He was angry with
him and wanted to make this clear.

"Listen," he said sharply, "first thing is 'you don't
argue with the law when they tell you to move. You
move."

"Sorry." The man looked shamed, embarrassed. It was
an encouragement to Atkins.

"Second thing," he went on, "you watch your mouth.
You pick your time if you've got something like that to
say. You don't tell the whole world. All right?"

Davies nodded. Still drunk, Atkins found a pleasure in
lecturing the man like this. He continued to do so for
some time as they walked the streets for a while and then,
hesitatingly, took a bus back to the block of flats where
his parents lived.

He might have dumped the man on any other day but
somehow the incident with the policeman had cast him in
a leader's role which he was anxious to retain. They did
not speak about the Crawley job again until they were
both safe in Atkins's bedroom – Davies sitting somewhat
miserably on the bed, Atkins sprawled on the floor,
sucking the top of a beer can.

In between sips he said, "Why did you tell me that?"

"Tell you what?"

"You know."

The man shrugged. He looked embarrassed again. He
said, "It was an idea. I just thought ... you know ... "

"Were you serious?"

There was a silence. Peter Davies looked at the thick,
parted lips of the man on the floor as if trying to gauge
what they indicated: interest or ridicule.

At last, half-convinced that he was not being laughed
at, he began, "All I was saying was that if a few blokes got
together ... "

And gradually, over the remaining cans of Newcastle Brown, and then over cups of tea which Atkins's mother made and left outside the door, Peter Davies revealed his own dream. It was stunningly unoriginal. His knowledge of the cash and carry store where he worked was careful but not meticulous; he had indeed made a study of the place over a period of months but from a theoretician's point of view: there were omissions in his outline which even Atkins was able to spot (each time he did so he felt clever as seldom before).

The dream Peter Davies had was not based on anything as flamboyant as Atkins's own vague need for self-esteem; it was more practical, less romantic. He wanted money. Had seen his employers deal widely in the stuff, use it daily like any other commodity which they stocked – like beans, like toilet-paper, like stacks of plastic spoons. He had seen this and developed a swift greed. The greed had led him to a theoretical analysis of the possibility of crime, and this had evolved into a first practical step when, visiting relations in Southwark, he met Greg Atkins and fell into the trap of believing what he said. He saw Atkins as a decent criminal. Suddenly he had a friend who could turn his dream into fact. And with a rare act of bravery he had risked making the approach and now his entire story lay before him like a guilty act.

Davies stayed to eat tea with the Atkins family, and over beans and sausages gave up a few details of his own background. His parents were divorced and he lived with his mother in a three-bedroomed semi in Crawley which they owned – residue of the divorce settlement. He had O levels in maths and English, was 23 years old and had been a stacking boy, then bookkeeper, that's all.

Atkins's father, who was a thin and worried man with yellowed eyes, was impressed by all this; he sensed a different style of friend and tried to ingratiate himself: pressing more food on Davies, laughing at his small, pallid jokes. Occasionally the old man recounted something from his son's past and this drew an open-mouthed stare from Atkins, and an unsettling silence.

The tea remained almost a friendly, pleasant meal however, and it was also a break in which the two young men could consider and decide upon what they should do next – if anything.

If the meal had gone differently – if there had been more embarrassing pauses or a difference of opinion over something, anything – the possibility of the Crawley job would later have been ignored. It was still at such a fragile stage.

But this did not happen. Davies maintained a shy, almost deferential attitude towards Atkins and refused to capitalize on the fact that at last he held the interest of the man. This confirmed Atkins's feeling of superiority and made the possibility of crime – or at least of thinking about it – a more attractive prospect.

So that as soon as they had returned to his bedroom after tea, leaving the old people to do the washing-up, Atkins said, "So you reckon a Tuesday would be best?"

Davies nodded. "Big trade day. Tuesday night just after it closes but before the cash van gets there at eight-fifteen."

They discussed this for a while and then Atkins felt that he was losing touch with some of the details so he went outside and told his mother to find some scraps of paper and a pencil. With these, he returned to his bedroom, closed the door and went and knelt by a cardboard box full of old records. He turned this on its side and rested the paper on it. After a few seconds' silent thought he wrote a figure one in the left-hand corner of the first sheet and then the date. The cardboard was not very good to rest on so he took out a record and used that as backing.

He said, "We'd have to get it right. Know what we want for a start."

Davies, almost breathless with excitement, sat on the bed and nodded. He watched the pencil and paper with great concentration. Had nothing to say for the moment, was overwhelmed by a sense that at last he had started something off, that here, now, they were beginning.

Atkins would have agreed. By getting some paper and a pencil from his mother, by writing a number one in the corner and the date he had done something, taken a first step; dreams became figures on a sheet, ideas were being marshalled. This was practical – an achievement.

"First thing," he said, turning to his new friend and pointing the pencil at him dramatically, "is we'll need some guns."

Davies hesitated, looked lost for one moment and then nodded.

Atkins took the pencil and wrote it down. First on the list: guns.

"Next … ?" he said.

Eight

Since Kind had watched Atkins stroking Jo's head in such a slow, taunting manner he had become deeply worried – even the man's refusal to let his son use the toilet had not disturbed him as much as that memory. As he tried to understand the basis of this new situation, tried to guess where it might end, the picture fringing his thoughts was of that small, careful hand caressing the shining black hair, touching the flesh at the neck. He writhed away from the picture as from a snake but could not escape it. The vulnerability of their position at the hands of these men was underlined many times by this vision and he felt weakened by it, obsessed by the fear it held.

A few minutes after Daniel had wet himself, Atkins came into the kitchen and recoiled a little at the smell. Half-laughing, apparently anxious to make a joke of what he had done, he allowed Jo to take the boy to the bathroom, and she went slowly not looking either at her husband or at her captors. There was an accusation in her silence which was intensified by the child's small, continuing sobs and this seemed to touch all three men remaining in the kitchen.

Atkins reacted almost angrily. Pointing at Kind, who remained sitting at the table, he said harshly, "You. Where's the nearest phone-box?"

Kind glanced uncertainly at his own wall telephone but Atkins snapped, "Not that one, stupid. I said a public box."

Kind almost flinched. He said quickly, "There's one about a hundred yards down the road. Turn left at the bottom of this street and you'll see it."

Atkins nodded. His pistol was still in his pocket and the butt protruded in an ugly, dangerous way. Kind could not help staring at it, and the effect of this attention seemed to make Atkins act more dramatically: he pushed back his anorak so that it was behind the pistol and then laid one hand carelessly on the butt. "If I used your phone," he volunteered, "I'd be daft. People can trace calls – did you know that?"

He was mocking Kind again. Also, he seemed to be showing off, perhaps for the benefit of his mute friend Reg, who smiled and flicked his eyes up to the ceiling in his own gesture of ridicule.

Kind said, "Yes, I see."

A silence fell, in which the two men watched Kind in an indecisive way, as if wondering what else to do with him – like he was a toy to be used but they were not quite sure how.

He grew tense, became aware once more that not only

was he a participant in this drama but he was also, in some undefined way, its audience. Several times in the hour or so since the men had entered his house, Kind had sensed that the leader was parading his anger or power in unnecessary ways: like hitting him on the head, letting Daniel wet himself. These were odd, brutal displays and they only confirmed his growing belief that the men were nervous of what they were doing, were perhaps uncertain of themselves and this situation. Again, the fear in this fact returned to Kind.

Atkins suddenly broke the silence. "What are you doing at home, anyway?" he said.

Kind shrugged. "I work from home."

"Doing what?"

The third young man, the one with the polite expression, suddenly appeared at Atkins's elbow and Kind glanced at him before answering, "I'm a writer. I'm trying to write." Still the hesitation, the reluctance to make the claim.

"Oh yes?" Atkins seemed interested. But Kind volunteered nothing more and a silence fell again. This time, three pairs of eyes watched him.

"Is anyone likely to phone up?" Atkins asked suddenly.

"I don't know. They might do."

"You don't answer if they do."

"No."

Atkins nodded silently. Then he said, "A writer, are you?"

"Yes."

"What's your name?"

Kind told him and the man still nodded as if considering this. He seemed reluctantly interested to meet a writer, gave the impression that he wanted to ask a little more and for one extraordinary moment Kind felt that their positions had reversed and that he was now the outlandish person, the celebrity. But just then there was the sound of the toilet being flushed in the downstairs bathroom and Jo suddenly appeared behind the three men. The moment broke completely.

Jo stood in the hall and as the men turned she said in a flat voice, "I want some clothes for him. They're upstairs."

Atkins seemed anxious to help this time. He jerked his head at the polite young man and said, "Go with her."

Kind watched the two go, and something about the sight of his wife walking upstairs with another man made his switch his eyes suddenly to Atkins. The expression on that man's face was unreadable; he too was watching the woman, child and guard but his eyes were quite bland, his features almost totally relaxed.

Turning his gaze to Kind once more he found him watching and there was a pause in which both men stared at the other's eyes. They became tense. Kind sensed that he had foolishly revealed his own fears and tried to look away – but when glanced back at his captor, drawn to do so by the continuing silence, he found him smiling. This seemed a confirmation – a hideous sight.

There was action then, a sudden bustle as if a lot was happening though in fact there was nothing more than a few orders to Reg to keep the gun on Kind and a rearrangement of clothing so that Atkins's gun did not show. Then he opened the front door and stepped outside. As the man went, Kind glimpsed sunshine and a few wisps of unimportant clouds. He saw the green front garden of the house opposite and thought he could make out a moving figure at the window ...

But then the front door closed and he was trapped again, a prisoner. It seemed so bizarre that only an hour before he had been absorbed in the job of eliminating unneeded sentiment from the lines of a short story. He realized suddenly that it had not been a good story after all; his perspective had quite altered. Now he recalled his own words and hated them. They seemed timid, coy.

It took Kind at least two minutes to understand that the first stage in his formula for a successful attack on the men had been completed. It came as a shock which made him nervous, made him glance at his guard to see whether he could tell that his heart was beating faster, that his breathing was suddenly difficult.

There was no sign from the man, only flickering eyes and a fractionally moving gun barrel.

Atkins had gone out. This left two men in the house, each in different rooms. It was now possible, feasible, than an attack could be made.

Kind coughed. He wanted to cover his nervousness, needed to force himself to think. Timing first. It would take Atkins two or three minutes at the most to reach the telephone-box – he might be there by now, might be dialling his number, getting his money out. And then? The number could be engaged, there might be no reply – possibly, even if someone answered there might be only the briefest of conversations: if Atkins was worried about phone taps he might hurry out his message and abandon the box as soon as possible.

Then there would be the walk back. Total time? Kind screwed up his eyes, tried to guess. Perhaps five minutes – at the very most. Five minutes.

Fright became a positive force, a presence in his stomach. He began trembling minutely and had to clench his fists (slowly, hoping the guard would not notice) to try and stop this. Five minutes, now less. He must act at once. Must do something. Now, at once.

Kind looked at the man called Reg and met his eyes. He smiled briefly, foolishly, then said, "Would you mind if I put the kettle on? We could have some coffee."

There was the slightest pause and Kind, almost desperately, added, "I promise not to attack you." He did

not care about the lie, felt only trapped by the decision he
had taken, frantic now to carry it through.

The man with the shotgun took moments more to
make up his mind. Kind could feel the seconds moving
away from him, could hear small movements upstairs as
Jo sorted out clothes in Daniel's room and prayed,
actually prayed, that she would not hurry, that she would
keep her guard up there for a few minutes more.

Reg nodded. He made a small noise with his throat and
this was permission to stand, to begin …

With careful, precise movements, Kind stood up and
stepped over to the kettle which was kept in the corner
just to the left of the man in the doorway. He checked the
water level and found it full. He switched it on, watching
from the side of his eyes as his guard backed away from
the open door and stood with his back to the opposite
wall so that he had more room to point the shotgun.
There was a distance of perhaps eighteen inches between
the muzzle of the weapon and Kind himself, who now
began to take down cups from the cupboard and a jar of
instant coffee from the larder just to the left of this. He
burned with an awareness of the gun, felt it turn with him
and follow every movement. In a mental picture he
turned and tried to grab the weapon, heard it go off …

Kind was appalled at the fear he felt. In theory he knew
that he might be quick enough to deflect the barrel before
the man had time to pull the trigger; when the kettle
began to hiss, say, when something minute happened to
attract the man's attention for the small part of a second
necessary to turn and grab. In theory he knew that this
might indeed be possible. Then he heard again the
imagined explosion, felt the shock of the sound booming
in the tiny kitchen, waited for the implosion of flesh, the
spray of scattered blood. He felt raw and exposed; he was
sensitive to all movements and sounds. He was frightened
and ashamed, knew that he must move, must do so

quickly or time would have deserted him – and yet – yet.

He walked slowly to the drawer under the kitchen sink and took out a spoon, hands toying only briefly with the dozens of blunt knives which lay there. He made sure that the guard saw him remove only the spoon. Then Kind returned to the kettle and began spooning out instant coffe. Four cups. The solicitous host. He almost smiled but then a new wave of fear took him and his hands trembled, he spilt coffee powder. The kettle began hissing. He must move now, now.

The fight would take perhaps twenty seconds, perhaps less. This was Kind's almost hysterical estimate as he stood with his back to the mute and watched the kettle with sightless eyes. Twenty seconds should be enough to take and deflect the gun, wrench it from the man's grasp, hit him hard enough to gain time ... Perhaps less than twenty seconds, perhaps ten. How long would it take the armed man upstairs to hear and come running? And would he bring Jo with him or abandon her until he knew what was happening?

Kind forced these questions on himself again and again as he stood waiting for the automatic switch on the kettle to click open, but each time he ducked the answers, swerved round, found himself fixed mentally so that he could no longer draw reasonable conclusions, could only face the unbelievable prospect of what he must now do.

The kettle began to boil and the switch opened. Carefully, Kind began pouring the steaming water into the four cups. Now. He would do it now.

He picked up one of the cups and slowly turned round to face the man called Reg. Their eyes met and Kind forced himself to smile, knowing that it was a skull-grin, an appalling travesty of friendliness. He said, "Do you take milk?"

The man shook his head.

"What about sugar?"

Again, the shake of the head. Kind froze with terror. There was nothing to do now, no more reason to stand poised like this with the cup of boiling water in his hand. He must throw it at the eyes, throw and grab. Must do it now, could wait no longer.

His hand was shaking noticeably now. The mute saw this and looked back at Kind's face, not understanding. Kind stood there, waiting for his own action, waiting for himself to begin. He began to shake badly, the mute staring in wonderment at this sudden tremble. And at last, as Kind still refused to move and simply stood there with the hot cup in one shaking hand, the mute seemed to understand.

In one movement the man raised the barrel of the shotgun until it was pointing at Kind's face, at the same time uttering a short bark and jerking his head to one side twice; his eyes were alive now with his own type of fear, perhaps because he saw the fixed, terrorized intensity of Kind's stare. He barked again, backing away the few inches which remained between him and the wall, raising the shotgun suddenly to his shoulder so that Kind was staring precisely into the black, ghastly mouths of the twin-barrelled weapon. The man's finger was on the trigger and he remained quite still

In a dream, a slow dream, Kind turned a little to the right, stooped, and placed the cup on the white table top. He opened his mouth to speak but, like the mute, had no ability then, no words. He swallowed and tried again. When at last he 'did speak the sound was hoarse. "It's all right," he said. "I won't do anything."

The mute stood there, waiting.

Kind repeated, "I won't do anything."

The barrel of the weapon remained trained on his face. Kind turned round and with ghost-like movements poured more water into the three remaining cups. Then he continued to stand there, staring at the cupboard door, no longer having the strength to face his guard, not daring to risk the slightest movement.

He felt that as long as he stayed like this the man would not shoot, no one would hurt him.

He remained standing with his face towards the cupboard, hands resting like revealed weapons on the side working surface where the steaming cups lay. When Jo and her guard brought Daniel downstairs in his new clothes Kind was still in this position. Jo stood in the doorway and looked from Reg to her husband and back again; when neither moved she slowly turned and took Daniel into the lounge. The other man hesitated, opened his mouth to ask what was wrong but then closed it again and followed Jo. Almost self-consciously, he took his pistol from his pocket, though he did not point it anywhere.

When Atkins came back in three minutes later he looked at Kind's frozen pose, looked at Reg and laughed.

Nine

Finding weapons was the most difficult problem facing Atkins when he began making preparations for the robbery over the days which followed his meeting with Peter Davies. Having convinced his new friend that guns would be essential Atkins had to provide them – Davies himself said he had never dealt with these things, would not know where to begin looking.

In fact, Atkins was very nearly in the same position but was too proud to admit it. For the first time in his life he was planning something large, something important, in which he figured as the leader – he took this role quite naturally through his claimed experience as a law-breaker; Davies wanted a leader and had found one. Atkins found a disturbing power, a moving attractiveness, in this situation and felt that his claimed knowledge of crime – and therefore his reason to lead – would be seriously weakened if he simply told the truth: that he had no guns, no access to them, no knowledge of them.

It was a problem which worried him a great deal, so much so that he put it one side and began concentrating on other details first.

Planning the robbery was an extraordinary experience for him: it remained real and yet not real. All the dreams and claimed stories, all the drunken boasting to sceptical but silent parents, had found a focal point in this scheme. He would travel out of town, find this store, would deploy what forces he could gather, take the cash he deserved (*deserved* – remembering the expensive ships, the elegant faces of the girl assistants who frightened him) and return to the smoke where familiar paths would confuse all pursuit. Atkins was at home with this theory, felt enormously contented to be planning a robbery of this kind – as if his life had been directed to this moment, had been created for it.

Sometimes in the evening, lying on his bed and listening to the gentle boom of the television in the front room and the softer sound of the one next door, Atkins allowed his dream to expand, to develop in the most attractive way. One robbery might become two, could finance others, could become a life-style which would be both fulfilling and rewarding. He had never bothered much with the cinema but once a girl had forced him to see *Bonnie and Clyde* and Atkins had been outraged by the film: it was the final, explosive victory of law which disturbed him, made him angry. Yet before that violent climax it had been good; there had been something carefree, something freewheeling. A good film until then. Atkins remembered it now and his expanded dreams took further shape and colour.

Instead of the problem of guns he concentrated first on personnel. This was in fact not much less of a difficulty but at least Atkins had a point at which to begin: Reg Daley, his mute friend.

He put it to Daley in the back bar of a small, dark pub where they were barely known; told him after just two sips of beer though he had planned to relax Reg first just in case. When it came to the point, though, Atkins was too excited to wait, simply poured it out the moment he guessed that no one else could hear.

Conversation between Atkins and Daley was a basic and yet immensely complex process which had grown without conscious effort over a period of years – since they had left school together. Daley's inability to speak was overcome by a process in which Atkins injected a small, continuous stream of questions into his monologues so that the other man could indicate with sounds and movements of his eyes and face whether he was following, agreeing, wondering and, occasionally, disagreeing. There were subtleties in the process which neither fully appreciated but Daley knew that he could reach no greater level of communication and understanding than with his friend Greg Atkins. It was this loyalty which made him nod and utter affirmative noises while Atkins sipped beer and asked for help in robbing a cash and carry store.

That settled, the two men got drunk together. Further discussion of tactics and problems seemed unnecessary for the moment.

A few days later, using a confusing system of double-talk, Atkins reported by telephone to Davies that things had begun to move. "One body on board," he said. "More to come. All right?"

"You'll need another one at least," said Davies.

"I know what I'll need."

"Sorry. I'll leave that to you. What about ... you know ... "

It was the question Atkins had not been looking forward to. Once more he felt that his new authority was under threat and it was no surprise to himself when he heard lies coming from his own mouth, heard prevarications and deceptions offered as reasons.

"I've put feelers out and I should hear in a couple of days. There's this one bloke particularly who's done it before. Done it for me before. He's a – "

"Will it cost much?"

The point had not occured to Atkins before. He hesitated, biting his bottom lip in the lonely isolation of a telephone-box (his parents were not on the phone) and repeated the question to himself: would it cost much? He had no idea. Had no money anyway, could maybe raise twenty pounds from his mother and a bit more from his father, not much. Reg often had a few pounds and there was fifteen to come from the barrow this Saturday ...

"How much have you got?" he asked Davies.

"Not much."

"How much?"

"Well – maybe fifty. Perhaps a bit more, I don't know."

"We'll need more," said Atkins quickly. "If we don't have more we're stuck. I thought you were putting up the dough."

The lie made Davies panic. He said, "There's this bloke I know whose parents are loaded. If we brought him in he could bring some cash."

"What bloke?" Atkins was instantly suspicious, frightened in case his leadership was at stake again.

"A friend of a girl I know," said Davies. "He's a bit of a funny bloke ... "

"What kind of funny?"

"Well he's not very pushy. Except he hates his parents like mad."

"Would he do it?" Atkins was still uncertain whom else to approach to take part in the robbery and Davies's description at once made him feel easier. The truth was that after taking Daley into the scheme he had sat down with a pencil and paper (this now seemed important) and tried to list the people he knew who might also be asked to help. When completed, this list was composed mainly of abbreviations or Christian names: Atkins realized without understanding the significance of it that he knew the full names of hardly any of his friends.

After drawing up this list Atkins had gone through the people one by one, imagining the conversation, trying to live through the suggestion and how each man might respond: Jacko would laugh, would make jokes as if it was not real; Bill, tall Bill, would not really understand; Bill's brother ...

One by one the names had been crossed out. Atkins's own imagination took him back to square one and he was left with himself, with Reg Daley and with a bloke called Peter Davies whom he did not really know and who had already made clear that he would not take part in the robbery itself, would be simply an inside contact.

Atkins had not considered how difficult crime could be. Reporting to Davies that he had one man on board had been a weak delaying move but now he was being offered a possible third gang member and a chance at least to fund the purchase of guns even if he still had no idea where to buy them. The arrangement was quickly settled, and they fixed for Davies to make the approach ("Carefully," warned Atkins. "Like I did it.")

Two days later all four men met in a pub in Coulsdon, roughly half-way between Crawley and Southwark. Daley and Atkins got there by train, the other two used an

Austin Maxi belonging to the new member of the group.

The man struck Atkins from the first as exactly the kind of person he would have expected to have rich parents. He did not know why. His fashionably casual clothes perhaps, or maybe the way he ordered bitter in a glass with a handle and a small Southern Comfort to chase. It was wrong. Delicate touches. On a pretext, Atkins got Davies alone at the bar.

"Are you sure about him?" he asked.

Davies nodded. "He wants in," he said.

"Why? What for?"

Davies shrugged. "Money, I suppose. I didn't ask – why?"

"I thought his parents were rolling in it."

"It's not the same."

"Isn't it?" To Atkins, who always 'borrowed' money from his parents, this seemed absurd.

Davies said, "It's not his own money. He wants some. Listen – he's all right. He'll help and he'll fork out to buy – " Davies glanced uneasily behind him and added quietly " – things. You know."

Atkins made a shrugging movement with his face. "What's he like anyway? What's he do? Does he work for his old man or something?"

Davies looked embarrassed. A slight flush crept into his pallid skin. "No," he said, and seemed reluctant to go on.

Atkins had to repeat his question. "What is he then? What's he do?"

"He's a student."

"What?"

"An art student."

"Oh Jesus Christ ... "

"He's all right. Honestly. He won't let you down."

"Listen ... " Atkins leaned closer and pointed. Then he hesitated, saw the weakness of his own position and gave up. "Come on," he said, "let's talk to the bastard."

Seated round a table the four men underlined their differences by the way they sat: Atkins sprawled in his chair, half-turned away from the others; Daley sat poised in the corner, forever dividing his glances between whatever interested him and each movement Atkins made – he seemed quick, yet still, his eyes burning, the creases in his cheeks marking him as an unusual man; Davies sat furtively, often looking this way and that as if studying the others in the pub; and the stranger, the newcomer, sat like a woman. This, at least, was Atkins's view. He remembered the incident in the underground walkway at the Elephant and Castle and watched the man with suspicion.

At last, Atkins offered the flat, posing statement he had prepared in the train on the way down.

"If you want in," he told the man, "you'll put up a hundred and fifty, cash."

The man nodded.

Atkins, aware of the respect, almost fear, which lay in the other's eyes, went on, "You also do what I say and you don't back out. You don't tell anyone – I mean *anyone*, especially not your arty-farty student friends – and when I say come up to Southwark and talk you come. All right?"

The man nodded.

As an afterthought, Atkins said, "And we may want to use your car for the job."

There was a surprised pause.

"Is that wise?" said the man. It was the first serious question and Atkins took it badly.

"It's wise if I say it is," he said angrily. "The way we're going to do this no one's going to see us come or go. If we start nicking cars for it we're asking for trouble even before we start."

"OK," said the man.

There was a silence. With the unexpected delivery of a

car into his power Atkins had solved yet another point which had been worrying him: he had only once stolen a vehicle and that had been for one hour when he was 15 – an offence for which he had been caught and fined by juvenile magistrates. Now he had transport, a full gang and enough cash to begin thinking about weapons.

"What's your name anyway?" he asked the student.

The man sipped Southern Comfort and said quietly that it was Harold Pointer.

After that, whenever Atkins addressed him he referred to the man as Harry-boy. They drank a great deal and at the end of the meeting Pointer took out a handful of ten-pound notes and counted out one hundred and fifty pounds. This money he silently pushed across the table to Atkins, who picked it up and put it into his own pocket. The transaction was completed quite openly, without a thought of secrecy.

Ten

Kind and his wife were washing up after lunch.

She was washing, he was drying up. Daniel was in his cot upstairs sleeping.

After the incident of the failed attack the atmosphere in the house had become more relaxed, as if Kind had been tested in some way and found to be no danger. He suffered for this thought but could not deny it; saw it in the way the mute now half-lay at the bottom of the stairs, guarding them from five feet beyond the open kitchen door instead of hovering over every move they made. Kind also sensed his failure in the looks the men gave him: or at least, two of them. The third member of the gang seemed embarrassed, shy of what was going on around him. He refused to look at Kind at all and was helpful to Jo in a polite way. He carried the food tray through to the kitchen from the lounge; Kind watched this and felt helpless, useless.

Now that their guard was far enough away for them to risk a little conversation under the distracting noise of the clattering plates Kind wanted to ask his wife what the men had told her, whether they had given any impression of how long they planned to stay. He also wanted to know whether anyone had seen them come in and whether anyone did plan to call at the house that day.

He wanted to ask all of these things but, taking plates, glancing in a hidden way at his wife's profile, was unable to bring out the courage to speak. As if sensing this, she broke the silence at last, though carefully, with a voice he had to struggle to hear.

"What are you going to do?" she asked.

Kind could not believe the question. He waited for a moment then said, "What?"

"I said – " her voice grew just a little louder, giving him the impression that she was only just keeping her temper "– what are you going to do? When are you going to do something?"

She was staring at her own hands as they moved in the water, scrubbed plates and withdrew them from the suds. Her eyes were without feeling, were completely blank.

Kind felt a little angry as well as frightened. He believed that his wife was being unreasonable and wanted to say so. Sometimes they argued very badly. Now, he just said, "Do what?" He realized how weak this sounded and became even angrier.

Jo said nothing for a while. She washed two glasses very slowly, rinsing them at the tap one by one.

At last her voice came again, this time almost trembling with suppressed emotion. "Daniel is upstairs."

That was all she said. It seemed an accusation and a

shriek of contempt. Kind fought against the feeling, tried
telling himself that she was being unfair, that it was her
own hysterical fear which was being voiced and not his
own. He tried forcing himself to be calm but failed. He so
much wanted to explain himself, to say that it was not his
fault, that he would do something, that she and Daniel
could trust him; could not though. It seemed too big a
thing to say, he knew he would not find the words for it,
would go on and on until the man with the gun grunted
out an order for him to stop and *still* he would be unable
to convince her. So he said nothing. They finished the
washing-up in silence and afterwards Kind felt that he
had wasted valuable moments.

When the kitchen was tidy and the plates had been put
away Daley shouted at them and indicated with a flick of
the gun that they should go through to the lounge. Jo
walked slightly ahead of her husband and at the doorway
appeared to shrink away from him in order to avoid
contact – or perhaps he imagined this. Kind raged at
himself, felt the accusation anew but could do nothing.

The lounge was a mess. Atkins was sprawled in the
armchair under the window in the far corner, the other
man sat at the table watching him. Open beer bottles lay
or stood in various parts of the room and there were
boot-marks on parts of the dark orange carpet. Some
cushions had been thrown onto the floor, apparently for
no reason, and the air was stale with a smell of sweat.
Kind and Jo stood in the centre of the room and waited
for orders.

At first, Atkins pretended not to notice them, simply
stared through the window at the roses which were
flourishing in red and yellow clusters on the broken poles
of the pergola outside. Kind noticed that a bird was
eating from the food-bag he had hung there – a wren, he
thought; he was not good at identifying birds. It was a
sweet creature though: quick and very pretty.

Atkins stirred at last and gave a deep sigh. He had taken quite a lot of home-made beer and seemed drowsy. He looked from Kind to his wife and back again, letting his eyes drop to her legs and then raising them again to her face. His pistol lay on the window-ledge in a careless, disregarded manner. He nodded towards the couch and said, "Sit down."

Kind automatically moved to do so. His wife followed only slowly and when she sat she rested her face in one hand and closed her eyes. Kind longed to take her hand and comfort her as he had done that morning, but he no longer felt entitled to do so. He looked back at Atkins and felt hatred rise above fear. This surprised him. He felt almost proud of it.

Conversationally, Atkins said, "We may stay the night."

Kind nodded. He knew that he ought to respond in some way, to encourage the man to talk because that way he might learn something, might even form a relationship which would make it more difficult for them to hurt his family if the time came for that. He knew this but remained silent, aware that at his elbow, unseeing, Jo followed every word.

Jo's voice took him completely by surprise. Without opening her eyes she said, "Why?"

"Because we're waiting for someone." Atkins seemed too tired to be angry – or perhaps he simply wanted to please the woman.

Jo did not reply for a moment. Then she looked up and said, "Why don't you just go? Go away."

A disgust and tension held her deep voice. It was an ugly sound. A sound of gross insult. Kind, watching Atkins, actually saw him blush and thought: What kind of people are they? What criminals?

From the table, the polite young man interrupted, perhaps aware that his leader was about to become angry.

Quietly, he said, "We'll go soon. We don't mean you any harm."

Atkins said nothing but stared at Jo with a new hostility on his face. Kind said, "What if we guaranteed to tell the police nothing about you? We could say your faces were covered … "

He saw Jo turn towards him and met her eyes. They were quite still.

There was a silence. No one dared speak and Kind was aware of precisely what this meant. He wondered whether, ever again, the correct formula might present itself, might allow him to regain some honour. Perhaps, he thought, if they were waiting for someone then Atkins might use the public phone-box again, and perhaps if that happened …

From upstairs came the thin, waking cry of Daniel. Nowadays he did not sleep much during the day but slept longer at night. His cry became a wail, a need for attention, and without bothering to ask permission, without even glancing at the three men, Jo stood up and walked out of the room. There was a pause. Kind waited for Atkins to order one of his men to follow her but that did not happen. Instead, after just a few seconds Atkins got up, picked up his pistol and began walking out of the room.

Kind leaned forward to stand but Atkins did not even bother to pause, simply waved to his friend who lifted the shotgun and pointed it at Kind's face. Slowly, he sat down. He heard Atkins reach the bottom of the stairs, heard him begin to climb.

Eleven

In the two weeks after the meeting in Coulsdon, Atkins spoke to Davies four times and became increasingly aware that the robbery they planned would be more difficult than he had imagined.

On the surface, Atkins already possessed most of what he needed; men, transport, inside knowledge and even a small amount of funds. He had managed to rationalize into an advantage the fact that none of them had experience of armed theft: they would not be suspected of the break-in, Atkins told himself; their escape should therefore be total once they had cleared the building itself.

Yet despite these real or imagined advantages, Atkins found many difficulties arising, some of them quite important.

Above all, it appeared that despite his claims to have all the information they would need, Davies had a far from perfect understanding of the protection systems at the store. He was not even sure about some minor points of lay-out and had to be sent back to check that a door existed here, and that it was possible to walk from one point to another without hitting a wall. Atkins, aware that his own grasp of detail had never been good, felt doubt and worry creeping in each time he found holes in Davies's understanding.

"I thought you said you'd worked all this out," he said at last as they sat in a Wimpy Bar and drank cold tea.

Davies shrugged and stared out at the traffic. "I have," he said. "It's just that when you put it like that I'm not sure ... "

"Jesus."

"I'm just not sure, that's all."

Atkins, watching the small blonde girl behind the till who was very pretty and who ignored him in an obvious way, came to a conclusion.

"We'll need a map," he said. "You draw one and we'll work it out bit by bit."

"A map?"

The girl glanced, then looked away with a set, ugly expression on her face. Atkins burned with embarrassment.

"A bloody map," he said. "All the doors and everything. Do something for your cut, for Christ's sake."

"All right."

"And it's got to be right." Atkins was furious.

"All *right*."

They were near to falling out many times. Atkins found himself trapped by detail, oppressed by it. The more he looked at the project the more work he found they had to do and the more time he had to spend alone on his bed staring up at the ceiling, imagining scenes, combating possible outcomes.

There were times when he was wrapped with claustrophobia at the prospect of continuing the project, that it would not let him go, that he was being drawn towards some point which would force on him its own conclusion regardless of the effort he expended in getting there. He became bad-tempered, and stayed away from the arcades and pubs where he was known, aware that the slightest word could now send him into a fury. Always short-tempered, Atkins had become so obsessed with worry that he was perpetually on the edge of rage. His parents suffered for it. His father was even moved to correct him once for shouting at his mother, but Atkins took this with a silence in which violence seemed to lie behind his eyes, and the old man backed away, mumbling.

Beyond all the detail of producing a correct plan, there lay the remaining worry of the guns. Atkins still had none, in fact had done nothing to produce any because he was simply frightened of making an approach to any person outside the small gang he had formed. There *were* people on the fringes of his life who might indeed have led him eventually (And for money) to a source of weapons. These were men whom he saw and recognized by vague reputation, by a kind of received knowledge of character – men with real criminal records, friends of friends of people he sometimes drank with or played pin-ball against. With work, Atkins might have met these men and persuaded them to take him further. But the reality of that work and the risks involved, the distance it would take him from his familiar paths of life, so frightened Atkins that he did nothing, kept the problem at the back of his mind where it added to the worry and the temper.

Davies did produce his diagram of the cash and carry store.

He sent it by post with a short, unsigned note written in ball-point: "As required. See you Saturday."

As required. Atkins glimpsed a different world there, admired the phrase. He spent several evenings in his room studying the drawing and found it reassuringly neat and detailed: exits and entrances were properly labelled and the writing was good, unlike his own which varied with his mood from careless to illegible. He felt more secure, more purposeful, when he stared at this diagram. In fact, it fitted precisely into the distanced mood of his dreams. On paper he could imagine his group of men driving down this road here – twin parallel lines in pencil – and stopping by this entrance and using this wall for cover ... all in theory, all as dotted lines and labels.

Davies came up to Southwark on the Saturday as promised in the note, and they spent the afternoon in Atkins's bedroom working out the details of the robbery. At the end of it, Atkins threw down his pencil and stretched himself out with his feet on the bed. Without bothering to raise his head he called for his mother to bring some tea and heard her shuffle towards the kitchen. He smiled.

"It's good," he said. "It's going to work."

"If we can trust everybody."

"What's that supposed to mean?" Atkins was feeling warm; he did not want doubts.

Davies shrugged. "Nothing really. The other two, I suppose."

"What?"

"Sometimes I just can't imagine them doing it."

Atkins sat up sharply, hating the man yet again. "Reg is all right," he snapped quickly. "You don't need to worry about him. *You* said the other bloke was all right."

Davies was silent, and Atkins looked at him and saw that the plump clerk was wearing an expression of regret. This infuriated Atkins. The point was that he too suffered from precisely that form of indecision, asking himself what it was he had got himself into, whether or not he ought to drop out now while he still could ...

But so far at least, Atkins had managed to control these feelings, and this was enough to enrage him when he saw the same symptoms indulged elsewhere.

"Bloody hell, you won't even be there," he exploded. "You'll be safe at home while us lot take all the risks. Why should *you* be worried?"

"I'm not worried."

"Sure!"

"I just – I just mean they *might*. I'm not saying you would. *You* wouldn't – "

"You – "

"Honestly. But if one of the others gets caught they might tell, that's all. That's all I'm worried about."

"Well tough. If one of us gets caught we all get caught. We're all in the same boat and it's too late to whine ... "

"I'm not whining."

A thought suddenly came to Atkins and he used it to attack the other man.

"Anyway," he said, "we take more risks than you whatever happens. Even if we do get away the first thing the law will do is button down everyone who works there and start asking questions – especially if we get away with it easy, so they reckon we might have been told. Know what I mean?"

"Yes." Davies blushed and looked away.

Slowly, now pointing a finger, Atkins went on, "So then they get around to you. And what do you say?"

"Nothing of course."

"Be sure about that though."

"I am sure."

"Yeah well are you?"

"*Yes* ... "

Atkins said nothing. But for one short, intriguing moment he just glimpsed what a pleasure it might be to nurture hatred, to have a cause to hurt this man.

His mother brought the tea then, knocking on the door first and waiting while Atkins shouted for her to come in. She placed the tray on the floor by the bed and smiled at Davies when he said thank you. Atkins said nothing because he was by now thinking over again what had just been said; somehow it had bever occurred to him before – or at least, not so that it mattered – that Davies might indeed by questioned by police. He bit his lip and wondered again just how clever he was being really ...

They drank their tea in silence and when Davies came to leave they parted on bad terms.

With Reg, Atkins was far more relaxed. In fact, now that they had a common purpose to bring them together their meetings were more exciting, more lively, than in the past. The tendency had been for their talk (as much as it was possible anyway) to be squeezed in between machine games or fast drinks. Quite often there would be nothing to say and this would embarrass Atkins; he would begin to feel uneasy if silences went on for too long when there was nothing else to distract him – no moving ball or flashing light. Now, there was the robbery to discuss and he talked about it at length, drawing strength from Daley's grunted approval and eye-flicking nods. At Daley's home:

"We're going to make money, Reg. We're going to make enough to last three years of normal living – that's without the barrow or anything. And if we *really* spent it should last a year at least."

Then:

"Or we could use it. You know, use the cash to get some more. We could set up something really good ... "

A pause.

"Did you see *Bonnie and Clyde*? I did. They just walked into places and took the money and walked out again. Great film. Mostly. I wish we had it that easy though. There's a lot to do on this one, Reg, it's ... I mean we've got to get it dead right."

Then:

"They were shot in the end though." Laughter. "I mean it wasn't that easy."

Nods. Grins. A good joke shared.

And then he held the first briefing session for the whole gang – that is, Reg Daley, Harold Pointer (who seemed to have learnt to ask no detailed questions beyond those which seemed both inevitable and polite) and Peter Davies, who was not to take part in the raid itself but sat pallidly interested like a sponsor watching those whose activities would eventually be beyond him. With this group – a mute, a timid student, a watchful clerk – it became inevitable that Atkins should not only dominate but shoud create for himself a situation in which all thought, all ingenuity, even all constructive criticism, had to be self-presented. This filled him with a mixture of elation, fear and frustration which in turn made his attitudes veer from the casual to the frantically angry.

It was an exhausting session for all of them. The

briefing was held in Atkins's bedroom and involved the use of the drawing Peter Davies had produced of the store. This was fixed to the cupboard door with drawing-pins and Atkins stood before it like a teacher addressing a crowd of worried examinees. He outlined the plan and then asked each man to parrot his own part in it. There were many mistakes and, ironically, the only one to avoid criticism was Daley who gave an account of his own part with a form of hand-play, gestures and sounds which meant little to anyone but Atkins.

At the end, Atkins told them all to go over their parts by themselves and to keep going over them until they knew *exactly* what they would have to do. They all nodded, including Davies, whose main job was to take them over the ground beforehand and make a last-minute check for changes at the store.

Pointer said, "It looks like a good system," and Atkins grew calmer.

"It is good," he said. "It'll work."

"And when do we divide the money?"

Atkins shrugged. "Next day. That night. I don't know – what do you want to do?"

The rare seeking of advice seemed to fluster the young student. "Well – " he began, " – I suppose I'd like it that night if we can."

"All right."

"You can come to my house afterwards if you like. It's not far away from there and my parents are abroad until August so we'll have the place to ourselves. There's plenty of room."

Atkins nodded. "All right. The three of us will divide it up there and I'll take Pete's for later. Any questions? No? Well don't forget to keep learning what you've got to do and we'll go over it again in three days. You've all got to know what you're doing by then. Understand?"

The others nodded quickly and this seemed to satisfy

Atkins still further. He made a few jokes and they laughed. He ruffled the student's hair and called him Harry-boy and the student looked a little red-faced which made the others laugh still more. This pleased Atkins. His mother gave them all tea and they were very polite to her, especially Davies, who was flattering about the decorations and the food.

Later, alone with Reg Daley in the pub, Atkins confided that he was feeling shagged out.

The other man nodded. Watched him carefully for signs.

The bar was exactly the sort of place in which Atkins had always felt at home – it was big and the floors were dirty, covered with a debris stretching back over months, trodden underfoot, ground into the tiles by crowd upon crowd. The walls were bare and smoke-stained, the only decorations a dart-board and some old receipts, now curling and brown like leaves, recording past collections for charity which had not been very successful. Everyone drunk out of straight glasses and no one ordered Southern Comfort. There were two fruit machines and the noise of them was perpetual, a comforting background like piped music, like a hum of crowded voices. This was what Atkins loved, where he felt most at home. He had not been to this pub for a while – he had forgotten why, prices perhaps – and now he regretted his absence. He felt warm. He felt useful. The afternoon's work seemed worthwhile, he felt entitled to this relaxation.

He told Daley a little more about how he felt, how the job might go and where the weak links might lie. They drank four pints of mild and bitter, sitting side by side on a hard wooden bench with their backs against the wall. No one bothered them; no one took any notice.

Occasionally, men came in who seemed to be outsiders, an indefinable difference which Atkins felt

proud to sense: the men did not belong in the bar, he and
Reg Daley did. The men drank up and left; Atkins
ordered another round and was served quite quickly. In
fact, he had not known a happiness like this for years,
perhaps not ever before. He was moved to touch strange
corners of his own mind and without looking at his friend
he said, "Reg?"

A small noise in reply. He recognized the tone of it, felt
good because of it.

"Do you ever get fed up? You know. Because of your
voice like?"

There was a pause, a long pause. In the end, Atkins
looked at the man, who smiled and shrugged twice,
quickly. He was dismissing the idea, pushing it away, but
Atkins held on. The mood was rare and to be used.

"I mean I go on at you, don't I? I go on and you never
get a chance to have a go back. You never want to *say*
anything, do you?"

This time, as Atkins watched, Daley only shrugged and
did not smile at all.

Atkins said, "If you got some money. You know.
Maybe you could do something."

Daley nodded. Smiled.

Atkins was drunk and suddenly felt that his eyes were
watering, and this embarrassed him. Daley looked away.
A silence fell and Atkins felt empty, felt almost that he had
trodden on something which was not there. He did not
understand. The silence irritated him and when a fruit
machine became vacant he suggested that they play for a
while. Daley agreed. They both invested two pounds and
lost it all.

Twelve

The silence which held the three men left in the lounge was fragile and anxious.

After Atkins had made his way upstairs the sound of all movement ceased, and even Daniel stopped crying; no one spoke, either in the lounge or in Daniel's bedroom. If Jo had said something or if Atkins had uttered a word, Kind knew that he would have heard because the walls of the house were very thin. He stared at the man with the shotgun and felt again the sharp, destroying tremble of hatred and fear. He was trapped precisely between a desperate need to get up and run to Jo and an equally ferocious sensation of terror – terror for the sound of a shot, for the sudden violence of it. Kind waited for a noise, a trigger to push him into action; he wanted a reason for insanity, a blanket with which to mask this craving for safety.

He looked suddenly at the timid young man seated at the table and found that he was staring out of the open door after Atkins, face strained for information: what was happening? Why had Atkins insisted on following the girl?

Kind could see the hesitation and dismay – yes, honest dismay – in the man's expression.

"Why don't you go up?" he asked suddenly. "Go on. You don't want to see her hurt, do you?"

The man appeared to fluster. "He won't hurt her," he said at last. "He's just gone up to make sure ... " His voice trailed off into uncertainty.

Kind became excited.

"You saw him stroking her just now," he said, his own

rage now turning to desperate persuasion as this new possibility of help became more real to him. "And you know what kind of man your friend is. Don't leave them alone there. Either let me go up and tell your friend to put his gun down or go up yourself. For God's sake, man! Go *on*!"

The young man jerked himself to his feet as if propelled by the force of Kind's demand. Then he hesitated again, and the mute had time to move his shotgun in a threatening gesture.

The man barked a short sound at his friend, shaking his head madly. He repeated the sound again and again, nodding now in a clear sign for the man to take his seat again.

Kind leaned forward and the gun came round to face him once more. "Go on," he insisted. "If I can't go at least make sure you're not an accessory to rape."

"He won't rape her." The words were anguished and unconvinced.

"That's exactly what he'll do," Kind half-shouted. "He's gone up there alone because he wants her. Christ, my 2-year-old son is up there. For God's sake do something!"

"I ... " the man began, but couldn't finish his reply. He stood with his mouth open staring over the head of his friend at the open door as if willing himself to move but in a frightened way, a timid way.

The tension became unbearable. All three men were now waiting for something to happen, either there in the room – panic or violence – or elsewhere, up in the bedroom where each ached to see what was happening.

At last it came.

There was a sudden shout from the bedroom – Jo's voice, raised in an anger Kind recognized exactly. More shouts then, and the sound of Atkins growling something – staccato, senseless words shot through with the intensity of violence. Kind stood and the shotgun raised with him, the mute also rising.

Kind turned to the other man and said quickly, "Go on or you're all accessories."

Now, at last, the man began to respond as if finally released from a trance. His own friend turned to cover him with a shotgun as he moved forward but he ignored it, simply hurried past and was suddenly out of the door beyond sight, unharmed. No explosion. No gunshot to deaden the ears. Kind heard him go and felt a blessing of relief, a wonder that something was being done, that this much at least he had achieved.

His guard stood uncertainly at the door, eyes flickering, now watching for the slightest movement as if perhaps determined not to be weak a second time. Kind, strangely unafraid, stood and did not bother to move but his ears followed everything that was happening elsewhere in the house, traced each sound and gesture.

He heard the young man reach the top of the stairs and turn right, running the few steps along the landing to Daniel's room; the sound of shouting voices there died suddenly, at a single moment, and the young man did not utter a word.

A complete silence held the house.

The man standing before Kind seemed completely lost; Kind, watching him, seeing the frantic eyes and deep facial creases, sensed for one moment the complete dependence of this man on his friend. In that second, he saw Daley as a pathetic man, actually found room for a moment's pity. This surprised him. It was the wrong circumstance for pity; Kind felt that it was almost a noble sentiment under these terms.

Upstairs, the silence was at last brought to an end by a low, unreadable murmur of male voices which continued for some while. The sounds were neither angry nor friendly, they were almost matter-of-fact as if the conversation was over some practical point, some details the men needed to discuss anyway.

As the conversation continued, there came the sound of footsteps – quick but frightened paces on the landing and now on the stairs. Kind recognized that this was his wife but felt no relief: the relief had come as the young man had ignored the shotgun and run upstairs, now it was replaced by a feeling almost of nervousness.

Jo reached the bottom of the stairs and Kind saw her at last, standing in the small hall holding Daniel tightly against her chest. The boy seemed frightened, alarmed. He had that expression Kind recognized very well, the look of a child touching an adult world and then stepping back in worried silence to absorb the feeling. Daniel would be the cause of no trouble for a short time now – he was watchful, subdued, taken up with whatever it was that had just happened upstairs. Jo, however, had a more active look to her face. She seemed both angry and upset and there was no easing of this expression when her eyes met Kind's over the shoulders of Reg Daley.

Kind said, "Are you all right, love?"

He did not move and neither, for the moment, did Jo. Daley half-turned to watch her but even he seemed uncertain as to whether she should enter the room or not. It was as if Jo worried him far more than Kind; as if, somehow, Jo was beyond the power of his gun.

Jo said shortly, "We're both all right."

Her tone was sharp. Kind began to walk towards her to offer some comfort, but Daley touched him once with the shotgun and he stopped. The barrel of the weapon rested lightly on his chest and the mute was only two feet from him. Kind looked at the man's thin shoulders; saw the weak, almost womanly hands on the stock and barrel of the gun and knew that if he moved very quickly now he could disarm him. Should he? Kind looked from the man to Jo and back agan. He thought of the last time he had

considered such a move – only an hour or so ago, yet
seemingly much longer; then, he had frozen through fear,
now ...

Now, Kind appreciated once more that the formula he
had set for an attack on these men did not exist. There
were two armed men upstairs and his own wife and child
stood between them. To despatch this single armed guard
and take his weapon would take perhaps five seconds.
This would be long enough for the others to hear and run
down the stairs.

By this time Kind might have run to the front door,
might even have the shotgun to hand – but he was not a
marksman, had no familiarity with weapons of any kind
and knew that it would not be possible for him to face two
men with pistols who would fire back at him.

Kind shrugged and looked at Jo, hoping that she would
take sympathy from his face and perhaps offer a little in
return. Jo appeared not to recognize the comfort he was
offering. She said, "Daniel wants the bathroom."

Kind nodded. He started to say, "Sure, you go ... "

But by this time Jo had turned and passed out of sight.
Kind heard the bathroom door shut quickly, and then the
sound of the bolt being pushed to. His overwhelming
feeling was one of frustration, also of unfairness. He was
estranged from his own wife, felt accused by her. He was
touched by rage which quickly faded to an empty fatigue;
Kind felt that he was becoming drained by the presence of
these men, that each of these confrontations diminished
him. What frightened him was the feeling that this
reduction might not be a temporary loss, that it might last
forever, was an ageing process which would not be
reversed by the removal of danger. Then it occurred to
him once more that unless he found some way of warning
the police or could deal with the men himself, it was
unlikely that on leaving they would allow him any chance
to repair his spirit, would probably kill his wife, child,

himself. The fear which he felt at this was completely selfless. It was a painful fear. He turned away from his guard and walked back to the sofa where he sat down with a carelessness which caused a sharp pain in his back. Stupidly, Kind had forgotten about the steel paper-knife in his belt, and now he shifted slowly to one side, keeping his face as clear as possible. There, this position was better, the knife no longer hurt him. He had been silly to forget it; had it dropped to the ground the man would have seen, would have guessed about that brief, wild fantasy which had taken Kind just seconds before he walked down the stairs and faced them for the first time. Would react very angrily, he knew that.

Kind stared up at the mute and, senselessly, smiled at him. There was no response, just a movement of the eyes.

The talking upstairs seemed to have been going on for a long time, but there were still no sounds of anger between the two men. Kind wondered what they might be saying to each other and how much the timid young man might risk standing up to his leader. It seemed improbable that he could put up much opposition.

The words – dull, muffled sounds still reaching him – sounded serious, detailed. The tones meant nothing to Kind. He could detect nothing from the sound except indications of a dry, perhaps important discussion. Of what? Possibly of Kind's own future and that of his wife and child: the thought came to him and the fear returned with a brief sensation of coldness.

There were feet on the landing suddenly and then on the stairs. Kind began preparing himself for some small attack which he felt he must deliver in order to halt this growing fatigue, this spiritual decay. He must make some effort now.

When Atkins walked in he seemed embarrassed to the point of defiance.

He stared at Kind, who saw that his colour was just a

little high – perhaps it was imagination, but this was unlikely. Atkins waved Daley to a table seat and stood there blocking the doorway so that his other friend stood uncertainly behind, waiting to come in.

Kind wanted to speak, but before he could say a word Atkins pointed a finger at him and said, "If I catch you talking to either of these two again – if I catch you doing anything I don't like – I'm going to break your fingers. I swear to Christ I'll snap your fingers off. You got that?"

It seemed an improbable, unnecessary threat.

Kind said, "What did you do to my wife?"

He said it firmly, was almost proud of the fact that Atkins's outburst did not sway him, did not make him cower.

Atkins strode forward now, putting his hand into his pocket and taking out the pistol which he pointed at Kind's face. His own expression was one of deep and sudden anger, but Kind felt that this too was a mask, that it concealed other feelings. Atkins said, "You don't ask questions, you bastard."

"What did you do to my wife?"

"Shut up!"

"I want to know."

"Shut your fucking *face*!"

The shout was so loud that it could have been heard in the garden. Kind wondered in the still moment which followed whether there was a possibility that such noises could be heard beyond the garden wall in the kitchen of the house at the back. He doubted it. There was normally very little noise disturbance between the two buildings.

The pistol was held in a straining hand which shook slightly. It was held fully outstreched in a manner Kind recognized as frightening at the same time as he realized almost in surprise that, for this moment, he did not care.

He said quietly, "Have you hurt my wife?"

Kind sensed the brutality of his own question, the

danger of it.

Atkins stared at him as if in disbelief. His mouth was open and his eyes seemed fascinated, bewildered. At last, he said, "No."

The tension in the room did not break, but it eased gradually from that moment as if draining from a bowl. Atkins lowered his pistol and stood there, giving the impression that he was uncertain what to do next. Then the man at the door walked in and quietly took a seat at the table next to the mute, who moved his shotgun and rested the barrel on the floor. Kind found himself guessing that it was a heavy weapon, difficult to hold at readiness for long periods of time.

Kind felt that he had a single moment's advantage, that somehow he had won a point, had taken a lead which would soon decrease and vanish. Knowing this, he forced himself to speak again.

"Why have you come here?" he asked slowly.

The other man muttered something as he turned away and took a sprawling seat in the corner armchair by the window.

Kind said, "I'm sorry, I didn't hear."

The man stared at him. He appeared to hesitate, and then he repeated, "I said why not? Here's as good as anywhere."

"Chance?"

The man frowned. "What?"

"Are you here by chance?" asked Kind, fighting his peculiar, almost funny sensation of disbelief.

The man said, "What's it matter?"

Kind shook his head. "It doesn't," he said. "It doesn't matter at all I suppose. It's just ... "

"Just what?"

"I don't know." Kind struggled for the thought and at last said, "It could have been anybody, I suppose that's it. It just happened to us."

Atkins thought for some seconds then turned to stare
out of the window and finally laughed once, quickly. It
was almost a shout of amusement, almost a cry.

"Yes," he said. "Yes it could have." Now he looked
back at Kind and the amusement was still there in his face.
"It's what I chose," he went on. "That's why it's you."

This seemed to please him, seemed to be important,
and Kind sensed in this resurgence of humour that his
own brief power was ending. He decided to use the final
moments.

"What *will* you do when you go?" he asked. He
recognized the danger of the question, that he might
prompt thought which might otherwise be ignored – but
there was this fractional recklessness on him, this brief,
luxurious contempt. He did not care.

Atkins was silent. He glanced at the other two who did
not offer a word or gesture of help. The pause
lengthened.

At last, when it seemed that he might never answer,
Atkins said, "We'll see about that when the time comes."

Kind opened his mouth to ask another question, but at
that moment there was the sound of the bolt on the
bathroom door being drawn back.

The four men turned their eyes to the doorway and
Kind was taken by a feeling that they were all nervous for
what Jo might say or do now. *She* held the power, and not
for seconds but forever. Jo's contempt mattered; her
feelings and glances were important not just to Kind but
to his captors as well. He recognized this with a jealousy
which surprised him.

In fact, Jo did not come through into the lounge, and
the men were left staring foolishly at nothing. Instead,
they heard her walk straight through to the kitchen, heard
also the small pattering, half-running sound of Daniel
following. No one moved. There was no pause now. As
soon as they heard Jo reach the kitchen the four men

caught the clear, unhidden sound of the telephone being lifted and then, in a slightly more frantic way, the noise of the first digit being dialled ...

Kind almost gasped. It was such a normal, everyday sound that for one moment he had accepted it as quite ordinary, quite without significance. Then this feeling fled and he realized what was happening: Jo was calling the police. She was calling for help and the three men were sitting listening as if they too accepted that this was her right, her normal function.

Two numbers dialled.

Atkins moved first.

He shouted one unclear word and began running for the door. At the same time the others at the table caught his fear and also launched themselves for the kitchen. The result was farcical, was enough to make Kind laugh had he not been held in a terrible suspension of hope: would she do it? would she have the time ... ?

In a struggle of shoulders and pushing, the three men sorted an order from their own chaos, an order in which Atkins charged through and the others followed. He was shouting. Kind jumped to his feet and ran after them, half-frightened, half lost in hope. As he reached the kitchen he heard sounds of a struggle.

Atkins was saying, " ... you stupid bitch. You put that ... "

Jo was saying, "Let go – let – go ... "

She and Atkins were fighting for the receiver. Kind stepped forward and began shoving the other two men aside in his attempt to reach his wife. Ludicrously, the men accepted his right to push them and fell away as if by order. He reached the struggling pair, sensed Daniel watching at the sink, reached up and took hold of Atkins's hand which held Jo's upper arm. He pulled, shouting, "Let her go, you ... "

At that second the barrel of the shotgun raked at his

face. It was bitterly cold. Not a hard blow, just an interruption, a complete halt to thoughts and feelings Kind let go of Atkins. Stood still, then backed away under a prodding from the gun, watching now as Atkins won the fight for the telephone receiver, plucked it from Jo's weakened hands and slammed it down onto the rest.

There was a sharp plastic sound. This noise was a complete end to the drama. All of them stood listening to the panting of breath. Jo looked down at the table and seemed held by anger or disdain or shock. Atkins stared at her and it was as if his eyes could not quite risk pure anger.

Kind wanted to laugh. This had been an impossible incident – also a foolish one because if Jo had run for the front door instead of instinctively seeking the telephone she might have reached safety. But still, she had almost succeeded even so. One second more and she would have issued her warning, if not to the police then at least to the operator. One second, and the three men had almost let her do it, had been frozen in turn by their own sense of normality. Kind actually wanted to smile; felt light-headed. Felt his own disdain for the armed men and their fragile power.

He said, "Let her go now."

Atkins still had one hand loosely on Jo's arm. He did drop his grip, but Jo looked up and snapped a glance at Kind which was a shock. There was no gratitude there, almost an accusation instead, almost a statement that he was intruding, that his help was not required.

This was a complete repetition. Kind felt that he was caught in some eternally circling drama, that he must play out this part, this weak and misunderstood part, time and time again in different roles. Scenes changed, their message did not. He wanted to shout out, to tell Jo not to be so stupid, to explain himself in ways which no one but she would understand. But he could not. These words

were not permitted, were not scripted. He had risked as
much as he dared and knew now that his only safety lay in
silence.

Jo started to push Atkins away, to walk out towards the
hall, but Atkins snapped a brief order and Daley put his
gun across her path. She stood looking down at it, halted
not by terror but by a simple recognition of circumstances. Why, Kind asked himself, did her
recognition seem to contain more dignity than his? It
seemed unfair.

Atkins said, "Well I've been nice. I've done what I can
... " He was still breathing heavily, not quite panting. He
hesitated and then went on, "Take them into the other
room, put them on the couch and keep them there – not
you."

The last words caused fear and pain to Kind. They were
spoken not to himself or to his wife but to Daniel, who
could barely understand. The boy had begun to hurry
forward to rejoin his mother (achingly, Kind recognized
that the boy, too, would have run past him, would have
preferred Jo's comfort to his own). Now Daniel was
halted by a firm hand on the shoulder as Atkins went on,
"The boy stay with us. We keep him upstairs in his room
and if there's any more bother – of any kind – the boy
suffers."

The statement contained all the menace Kind had
feared, the worst of the threats he had imagined. He said,
"Leave the boy with his mother ... "

But he was interrupted by Jo herself.

"Don't touch the boy." Her voice was trembling –
anger though, not fear. Kind heard and looked to Atkins
for defeat.

Jo repeated, "Don't touch the boy. Don't put one hand
on him or I'll kill you."

It ought to have been a pathetic statement but was not,
was quite powerful.

Kind, watching Atkins, not daring to add his own words now, saw just one moment's hesitation and thought Jo had won. Then Daniel himself broke the purity of emotion which held them all. He said, "Mummy ... " and tried to break free from Atkins's grasp.

The result was inevitable. Atkins hung on more tightly, Jo started forward and brought up his pistol to the child's head. There was an intensity here that Kind had never known before. The sight – gun to child's head – was beyond comparison, was ugly beyond sin or description. It simply should not have been, should not have been.

Jo stopped at once.

Atkins said, "I mean it."

There was a pause in which no one knew what to do, all looked for oders to the man with the struggling child.

He said, "Into the lounge. Sit down on the couch. Stay there."

Kind turned at once and found Jo staring at Daniel. The sight was a pain. He touched her gently on the shoulder but she moved back as if in fear of him. Together, though not together, they made their way past the other two men and into the lounge. There, they sat at opposite ends of the sofa like shy lovers. They heard Daniel call out three times as he was taken upstairs and placed in his own room. He was obviously struggling and it seemed that Atkins had trouble shutting the door on the child. Once shut, of course, it opened again – Atkins could not have known that 2-year-olds can open doors. It must have surprised him Again, Kind recognized humour but did not respond to it. He wondered how they would keep Daniel in the room, because there was no lock on his door. He wanted to say something, to speak to Jo. He was a short-story writer, a man of visions and sentimentality. Earlier that day he had struggled for the right words, the right phrasing. He had been absorbed with concepts of love and its correct expression in a piece which might sell for one hundred and twenty pounds, perhaps less. This was how he had formed his life. What he was. It seemed so silly, so pathetic, so pointless now.

Thirteen

The robbery was planned this way.

The cash and carry store was situated on an industrial estate on the fringes of Crawley, immediately alongside a big service road which led, eventually, to the A23 and to the motorway, the M23. It had been Atkins's original plan to use this motorway to escape back to London just as he had dreamed and boasted of many times; yet in momentary indecisiveness at the first briefing he had agreed to go to Pointer's house near Brighton, twenty miles in the opposite direction, immediately after the robbery: it seemed a shame later, a betrayal of much emotion but irredeemable. Atkins did not wish to give the impression that he often changed his mind so, after the raid, they would use the motorway to go away from London towards the coast and there they would divide the money.

The raid itself was supposed to be simple and quick. The plan was timed from the fact that trading finished at seven-thirty on Tuesday evening and that the cash from five check-outs was then collected into one office fifteen minutes before a security van arrived to take it away. This office, Davies pointed out (and drew in neat pencil lines with clear labelling), was a glass-walled room situated at the back of the main store as far away from the front entrance as possible. There was a safe in the room but the money was not kept there – at least, not just before the security van arrived. He had seen it himself, money ranged in bags on a table, waiting to go. In fact, it was exactly this sight, this glimpse of fortunes beyond all scope of his own salary, which had prompted his dream and vision and which led him to approach Atkins through a wild and uncharacteristic sensation of irresponsibility. Money in bags. Ready to be scooped up. It was enticing, irresistible. A dream of fine and contagious colours.

The security van always arrived at eight-fifteen and the two guards entered the vast store not through the main entrance, which was security-locked, but by a small, private side-door which led into a corridor just thirty feet from the glass-walled office. This door was unlocked by an assistant manager only after visual confirmation that it was indeed the security men outside (a spy-hole in the wood; Davies said he presumed they had some coded signal, but he was not sure. Anyway, it was not important).

The whole theme of Davies's plan – the idea which he gave to Atkins and upon which the robbery was based – was that although this door was locked and although it could not be secretly unlocked from inside without alerting management, Davies knew that the door itself was weak. He had tested it with his shoulder when no one was looking; had done so many times and felt the wood rattle, heard the lock start to give. And the outside protective alarm system would not be switched on until everyone had left the building. As Davies had put it to Atkins on the day they first met, "One kick, two maybe, and you're in."

It seemed absurdly simple but it had appealed to Atkins on grounds of rightness: one weak door guarding so much money? Why not? It was how these things ought to be.

Once inside there were two things to do at once. One was to enter the glass office and prevent the use of the only outside telephone lines in the building (telephones elsewhere were for internal calls only); the other was to throw the main power switch governing one quarter of the store – the quarter which included the office. By doing this, Davies pointed out, the main alarm buttons would be rendered harmless and though there were others in different parts of the building it was almost certain that a quick entrance and departure would be unnoticed by anyone except those in the office itself. There might be three men in the room, Davies said. The problem was to keep them quiet long enough to get in and out. Atkins said that two men with guns would make them lie on the ground and by the time they risked standing and found a working alarm button the escape would have been completed.

Pointer's job was to kick open the door together with Daley; Atkins was to stand back with a sledge-hammer for the lock should this prove ineffective (Daley had already stolen a hammer from a building site; it weighed fourteen pounds and Atkins had it in the cupboard at the end of his bed).

Once inside the building, Pointer was to turn left, locate the main power switch and shut down the electricity. Meanwhile, Atkins and Daley would run to the office and carry out the robbery. Atkins pointed out many times that the plan relied on speed. The car engine would be left running and he would drive; he insisted on that.

Other details which were finalized over the series of meetings in Atkins's bedroom included routes to and from the motorway – again, Davies provided the map – and an agreement that each man should provide his own face-covering. Pointer suggested that the number-plates on his car should be covered immediately before the robbery: he proposed using Blu-tack and some stiff white card which he could take from college.

With this plan, Atkins hoped to steal forty-five

thousand pounds, perhaps more if the store's takings had been especially good. Divided four ways this would mean equal shares of eleven thousand, two hundred and fifty pounds. Atkins, however, said that he should receive an extra payment and would take twelve thousand pounds. He had not worked out what share this would leave the others and neither had they.

Atkins warned his men to carry no wallets on the day and to wear "ordinary" clothes, also gloves.

This was all. At this stage, one week before the event, there was still the unsettled matter of the guns – a nagging worry which caused Atkins many wasted hours of guesswork and dejection. When, finally, he did arrive at a solution, it was through the same mixture of chance and stupidity which marked the whole plan and it was done through Reg Daley.

This man somehow guessed that his friend was worried about buying guns (though this had never been admitted) and felt deeply enough about the problem to keep his eyes open for a solution. In its way it was a touching affirmation of friendship and Atkins seemed to be aware of this when Daley met him in the Wimpy and instantly, indiscreetly, began signalling that he had something important to say.

Seated with his back to the vast front window, Daley leaned forward and crooked his hands into the clear impression of a pistol, shooting his friend several times in the chest.

Atkins was almost alarmed. "What about them?" he asked.

Daley jerked his head to one side and continued to indicate pistols until Atkins stopped him with a quick hand.

Hardly believing what he was being told, Atkins said, "Where?"

Again, there came the flick of the head, the nervous

eyes and, this time, two short vocal notes which Atkins recognized without effort. He stared and felt an immense and unquestioning sense of relief, also of affection.

"Right," he said, "let's just finish my tea." Tea was cheaper than coffee; Atkins had been dreaming of how unimportant these small differences would be in just one week. He swallowed the hot liquid and scalded his throat, and then stood to follow his friend out into the busy high road.

They took a bus. Went first to Atkins's home where they collected the one hundred and fifty pounds which Pointer had handed over in the pub and which Atkins had kept in the cupboard along with the fourteen-pound hammer. Daley tried to indicate that this was too much money but Atkins frowned and, for once, did not really understand.

They went to Camberwell Green. Daley was unused to leading his friend like this and began to get excited while Atkins became nervous and watchful: how, after all, had Reg met someone with guns? And what sort of people would they be?

They took a side-road and turned left and then right. By this time they were in the sort of dingy side-streets which somehow Atkins had always imagined would be the right setting for buying weapons: there was a watchfulness about the silent, terraced houses, a fatigue and carelessness in this abandoned car, this old man sitting on a broken wall, staring ...

It seemed frighteningly right, though Atkins had never considered it in detail, had only tasted the outlines of how it should be.

And now, at last, he glanced at his friend and began asking questions.

"What sort of a bloke is it?"

"How much will it be?"

"How many can we have, Reg?"

No answers, just jerks of the shoulders which Atkins recognized with fury and hysterical amusement as dismissals – not rude but excited. He forced himself to laugh. Said, "You old bastard."

Now there was a small line of shops – the sort which grow up well away from main streets: paint peeled; produce was grimy, prices high. There was a greengrocer's with a poor display in old boxes; a sweet-shop with old Easter-egg boxes in the dusty window; a terrible old second-hand shop with a hand-painted sign outside – *Goods Bought and Sold*.

Daley stopped suddenly.

"What?" said Atkins, caught by surprise.

His friend pointed and, frowning, Atkins turned to look. He saw it at once. Felt delight and then surprise and then anger.

In the dirty window alongside an electric iron and some pairs of walking boots were two replica pistols on brightly coloured boxes. At first Atkins had seen them as the real thing; one second, and he realized his error.

He turned in anger. "You stupid bastard!"

Daley, who had been smiling, stopped at once.

An old woman passed and Atkins could barely suppress what he had to say until she turned into the sweet-shop. The door emitted a single, clear bell note as it opened and closed.

He plunged on.

"They're bloody toys," he shouted, "replicas. Look, for Christ's sake, it says so on the boxes ... "

He fell silent again because his friend was nodding – earnestly, intently. Atkins began to feel that he had missed the point and he waited for some seconds before asking, "What are you on about?" Less anger now, more curiosity.

In reply, Daley crooked his fingers once more into the pretence of pistols and made shooting movements. Then he shrugged.

"What?"

Daley shrugged again. He pointed at the boxes and shrugged a third time.

At last, Atkins understood what he was trying to say. His face crinkled into disbelief and then, slowly, began clearing as the possibilities were imagined, tasted and found real.

"Just fake it?" he asked.

Daley nodded delightedly, quickly. He was so agitated now that he was almost jumping on the spot and Atkins had to reach out and touch his shoulder for one moment in order to calm him.

"All right," he said. "Just a minute ... "

Atkins turned back to the window and stared again at the two pistols on display. It *was* possible. It would be difficult to explain to the others but perhaps he could make up some story, explain it away somehow. The weapons did look real. There was an ugliness to them, a threat in the squat blackness of the bulbous chambers, in the snub of each barrelled nose. Atkins imagined hefting them, pocketing them, swinging them out and giving orders ... Yes, they would look real. They would frighten people and this, after all, was what he needed.

He looked at Daley and grinned. The mute caught the smile and answered it with a sound which was half scornful, half elated. Atkins punched him on the shoulder and he ducked and bobbed and threatened to hit him back. The old woman came back out of the sweet shop with a bell noise and found them sparring and laughing. She walked past carefully and timidly and Atkins almost stumbled into her but did not notice.

Inside the second-hand shop he was more subdued. He felt a little embarrassed and guilty buying the weapons, which cost ten pounds and were wrapped for him in an old brown vegetable bag. The two men took them home and played with them for most of the afternoon.

Fourteen

Kind heard Atkins destroy the telephone. It seemed a
surprisingly difficult thing to do and when the wire came
out it must have done quite so suddenly because there was
a sharp crashing noise and Atkins swore loudly. Kind,
obsessed now with the pieces of farce which seemed to
cling to each action of these men, actually laughed out
loud and glanced at Jo for an answering smile, but
received none. He felt quilty at once. That he could laugh
under these circumstances after all that had happened,
after what they had done to his son ...

From Jo's expression he could tell that she was
suffering badly, that perhaps she was near to some
breaking-point he could not imagine. Perhaps his own
breaking-point had been fear in the kitchen when he had
been unable to turn and face the barrel of that shotgun;
perhaps the moment was over for him now. And Jo? For
all Kind's sentimentality he felt left out of the emotion she
must now be suffering. He knew that he could be a
phlegmatic person sometimes; this was the plodding side
to his nature which Jo had identified soon after their
marriage. It could madden her – perhaps was doing so
now. Kind realized with surprise that the other side of
him – the part she called "fiery" – was probably all that
saved him, all that made his wife love him. The thought
came to him quite suddenly and he sat re-examining it for
some time, wondering if he was right to do so, or if this
might not be a trick he was playing on himself because he
was trapped, because his family was under threat. He
must do something, This too he understood.

Daniel was wailing upstairs – a slow, untearful but perpetual sound of irritation and unhappiness. The boy was also trapped. He wanted his mother. Did not call for his father at all.

Kind said quietly, "Daniel's unhappy."

He was playing for Jo's sympathy in an obscene way, but all that happened was that she glanced silently at him once and the young man at the table said, "Please be quiet."

Please be quiet. It was absurd. He held his pistol like a toy and pressed his knees together like a woman. And this was their guard. This, the criminal hiding for some reason Kind could not even guess at. Absurd.

Kind looked at him and decided that it was impossible to be afraid of this polite young man.

"What's happening to the boy?" he asked.

The man shook his head quickly, obviously scared that his leader might hear and object. But Atkins seemed to be busy still with the telephone or what remained of it, so Kind repeated his question a little louder, forcing the man to respond.

"Reg is in there with him," said the young man at last. "He's all right. Just don't say anything or do anything, please."

Kind nodded and a silence fell once more.

Glancing carelessly at his watch Kind saw in surprise that it was three-thirty. The men had taken them prisoner at about eleven-thirty and this meant they had been held captive for at least four hours; in fact, he reflected, it was surprising and yet not surprising. It seemed an immensely long time to be imprisoned and such a great deal seemed to have happened, and yet it was barely half a working day. At the insurance company he would now be sitting down to coffee in the managerial canteen; if today had been normal he would have been upstairs working, would have heard the small click as Jo switched on the electric kettle, would have waited for the knock on the door and the handing over of biscuits and a cup. Patterns. Broken with that first call up the stairs from a worried voice; shattered beyond recognition with all that had followed.

Kind felt restless suddenly, felt old and stale. He wanted to get up and walk about, wanted to argue, to say things, to use his hands in some way. He wanted everyone to understand him, to know that he was not a coward, not a dull person.

Jo was now biting the knuckles of one fist. Her skirt was pulled up just a little and Kind could see her knees which were very attractive. He wanted to tell her to hide them, to pull down the skirt because this was a provocation to people like Atkins, but he knew that even this statement would be misread, would be a defeat for him. Anguish and a desperation close to anger rose once more in his spirit and he could not for anything recapture that calm which had led him, just moments ago, to laugh out loud.

Daniel continued to whine. Perhaps it was this – this perpetual reminder, this abrasion on ancient instincts.

He said, "Look, why can't his mother go to him?"

The young man just shook his head.

"Why not?" demanded Kind. "She can't do any harm for God's sake. There's three of you with guns – what's she going to do?"

He felt Jo watching him now; felt proud at this.

The young man stared at his own pistol and gave a small, out-of-place smile. He looked a child, a young, appealing child. He said, "Your wife almost phoned the police."

As if in answer, Atkins suddenly appeared in the doorway.

"I thought I told you to keep them shut."

The young man did not look up, just said, "Sorry."

"Yeah."

Atkins stood indecisively for one moment. He looked

across at Kind and said suddenly, "Well you're not going to make any calls from now on."

"I gather."

Again, it was the wrong reply. Atkins seemed to hate the faintest taste of cynicism or sophistication on another's tongue – perhaps he confused the two. Whatever it was he now pointed at Kind and said, "If you cause any trouble, Reg upstairs starts laying into your kid."

Jo looked up and Atkins dropped his hand and met her eyes as if challenged to do so.

"Yes, lady?" he said. The words were ugly. Demanding.

Jo said, "If you touch him … "

"Yeah, yeah I know. You'll do me in. All right, lady, you've said your bit, now shut your mouth. Both of you."

It was as if Atkins needed to reassert his authority, Kind noted. As if he felt subtly beaten by Jo's earlier threat and needed to force this scene to demonstrate that he was untouched by it, was still in charge in all senses. Kind thought about the few words the man had sprung on them and wondered at the ease with which he could accept the threat to his own son.

What could he do?

No one had called, no one had tried to telephone (and even if they did phone now they would at best just report a malfunction to the operator). There had been perhaps one moment to attack these men and he had passed up that opportunity, had been too afraid to do so. Since then they had ordered him about and the closest he had come to rebellion was persuading the polite young man to run upstairs and stop his wife being raped. Now, Kind felt laughter rising again, but at himself.

Atkins had found some home-made wine in the bottom of one of the bottles; it was clouded with dregs but he did not seem to notice or care, just tipped it straight into his mouth. Kind winced then hated his own sensitivity.

Atkins threw himself down in the chair and stared out of

the window again. The afternoon had warmed and it would have been good to sit in the garden, to have felt the hot rays on naked flesh like water. Once more, Kind felt trapped, felt dirty just to be inside. He should be out there, should be rid of this cloying, exhausting emotion. He coughed. Atkins looked at him and Kind felt timid once more. This forced him to speak.

"Your man Reg," he said. "What happened to his voice?"

It was a stupid, unnecessary and dangerous question but Kind had stepped subtly beyond sense.

"Mind your own fucking business." Drawled yet angry words.

"I just wondered."

"I warned you."

The man stood up again and Kind felt cold, felt afraid for Daniel.

"What?" he said.

"I warned you to shut up."

"Richard!" Now it was Jo's voice, cutting in with swift power. "Leave it alone. There's no sense in saying things like that."

Was there the slightest pressure on the word "saying" ... ?

It was another accusation, a tired but frightened one. Kind looked up at Atkins and said, "Sorry."

"You fucking better be."

"I meant no harm."

"He's worth about ten of you lot." Atkins was becoming worked up, was emotional. "He's had people poking fun at him all his life for that. Cunts like you."

"I simply asked."

"How would you like me to start asking about your little boy, eh? How would you like me to go upstairs and start asking questions of my own? You want that?"

"No."

"You sure? You want to say something else about Reg you say it now and I'll go and see your boy. You say it. Go on."

"I've got nothing to say. I'm sorry."

"You be that."

Kind said nothing and the man continued to stare at him. His pistol was in his left hand but he was pointing with his right: a sharp, accusing, waiting gesture. The silence went on and Kind was at last forced to repeat, "I'm sorry."

This finally seemed to satisfy the man. Slowly he lowered his hand and, still looking at Kind, sat back down in the armchair. Atkins continued to stare until Kind lowered his eyes and even then he could still feel the white of his face turned towards him like a glare. He kept looking at his own hands. Hated this new defeat. Felt alienated from everyone in the world, like a sick man, a madman.

And yet. Yet it had been an extraordinary scene. From the smallest of insults Atkins had built a monument of affection, of protection; perhaps he too, like Kind, was prey to sentiment, was a fiery and a dull person. The echo of the man's temper held them silent for a further quarter of an hour and at last even Daniel gave up crying and a total quiet gripped the whole house. When anyone in the room moved – shifted position, crossed legs or sighed – it was a wild statement, a shout. Emotions smouldered like heaped-up fires and the silence rose like smoke, hung in the air, tainting it. Beneath its choking gases, each person was changed and turned, was fired into something new.

An odd, unbelievable time.

When Atkins at last looked at his watch and said, "Right," it was not an ending but a beginning. Kind felt it, knew that something inevitable must happen, would do so. Heard almost as an afterthought the man tell his friend, "I'm off to try Pete again. You keep your eyes on these two."

"Right."

It was all as it should be. Kind felt no surprise.

Atkins walked quickly out of the lounge feeling in his pocket for some change which he seemed to find. Kind heard him run quickly upstairs and wondered yet again whether he had remembered to hide his pistol, whether someone passing might glance in and see ...

Almost certainly not though. It seemed that this man loved details of this kind, discovered them as loving parts of some unfamiliar structure and nursed them for dear things. They were the sum of something new to Atkins, Kind was quite sure of that now: the moments of unnecessary temper, the flashes of power ended by embarrassment or shock – these were new to the man and this was perhaps fortunate: a little more intimacy with violence, Kind believed, might have created more danger. Or perhaps less. He was not sure.

He heard Atkins open the door to his son's room, heard a small shout of laughter. Why? Good or bad? He glanced at Jo and found her staring at her own lap but not seeing it; she was up there following each sound too, was well beyond this room and any touch of comfort Kind might offer. How odd that it should take this threat to force them apart. Kind heard himself sigh. Watched his breath move the hairs on Jo's temple; saw her fail to notice this or respond.

There was a single low voice upstairs, a monologue tilted with a cadence of questions – always unanswered. Reg the mute; makes Atkins angry just to hear.

Feet on the stairs again and Kind felt the sound like a drum roll, like a prelude. He knew exactly what he must do now and felt an odd, hesitant tremble in his body though not of fear, not quite of that, no; it was an actor's fright, a performer's hesitation. Not fear but anticipation; a guessing, or knowledge, of events to come.

Atkins put his head round the door and said, "Right?"

"OK." The young man with the gun twisted round quickly as if afraid of looking impolite.

Atkins glanced at Kind once more, seemed to hesitated – almost as if sensing something in the silence or fine tremble. Kind waited. Met his eyes. Wondered what the other now saw. And the pause ended, the hesitation was swept away by necessity – to ring this Peter, to finalize whatever business remained – and Atkins turned and left without a further word.

They heard the front door open, heard the latch slip down so that it would not relock, and then heard Atkins pull it shut and walk out into the street. Gone.

On earlier time estimates Kind knew that he now had approximately five minutes. As an introduction he leaned forward and sighed deeply as if in relief. He said, "Jesus, that man makes me frightened." Neither Jo nor the young man said a word and Kind knew how weak this made him seem but no longer cared; he was acting. He wanted everyone to become used to movement, this was important.

Fifteen

The night before the raid all four men gathered for a final briefing in Atkins's bedroom. Outside it was raining, and occasionally the wind gusted sharp bursts of noise against the window. It had grown dark early and the mood of the night exactly matched the subtle, sombre expectations of each man present: they were at last frightened of what they were about to do.

Atkins sprang his lie on them.

"One problem: I've been had," he said before the final rehearsal could begin. The men stirred, looked at one another. Atkins paused and went on, playing the embarrassed man, "I've got the guns – two of them – and everything went just as we planned. I paid a hundred and fifty cash and picked up the stuff in a pub down the road. Only they're not guns."

He paused again, still anxious to avoid the real deception.

Harold Pointer broke the silence. "What are they?" he asked quietly.

"Replicas."

"Jesus."

The word was quiet but it stung Atkins. He had been expecting to pay some toll in accepted abuse or mockery but now that the moment had arrived he found himself unable to do so. He became angry.

"Listen," he half-shouted, pointing at the student, "they're exactly the same as real ones and I was given them in a bag in a crowded pub – there wasn't time to do more than take 'em and run. If *you* reckon you could've done better – "

"I'm not saying that."

"I was let down. My mates gave me a wrong man. I've bollocked them and they've gone looking for him but it'll take time and we haven't got time."

"Right."

The others all made agreeing noises, even Reg who knew the truth. The three men seated on the floor round Atkins's bed were now trying to calm him, to soothe, to say that yes, they also would have made this mistake, that there were bastards everywhere and no one could be trusted. No one dared risk a joke although, on one level at least, it was quite funny.

At last, someone had to ask the inevitable question. Peter Davies coughed in a sudden silence and said, "Is that it then?"

"Is what it?" Atkins was only half-truculent by now.

He was glad to have the ordeal behind him but could not let go of his bad temper too soon or the others might have become suspicious.

Davies shrugged. "Do we pack it in? Without the guns – well, should we stop?"

Oddly, the pause which followed was not tense at all; neither was it full of horror or rage or even despair. If anything, it contained a hope no one dared voice.

Atkins, prepared for this moment, said gravely, "We go on."

"How?"

"We pretend. They're good fakes. We fake it. Who'll know?"

No one could answer the question, or no one risked doing so. The men looked at one another and there were a few tentative smiles, grins of encouragement. Then Pointer raised one hand as if at school seeking permission to speak. Atkins gave it with a nod.

"I've got – well, my father's got – an old shotgun. Not a bad one actually. And I think there's still some cartridges somewhere about the place. I could have a hunt round if you like. I'm sure we've still got the thing tucked away somewhere."

Atkins stared at him in silence for a moment. "What kind of place do you live in, Harry-boy?" he asked.

The student blushed and grinned. A childish sight. "Actually it's a bit of a rambling dump," he said. "Bags of room."

"How much room?"

Pointer coughed. "Oh – about fifteen acres, I think; mostly scrub."

"Oh yes."

There was a further silence.

Rain shook the windows. It felt warm in the room but small. Small compared with fifteen acres. Southwark held no comparison; they measured nothing by acres in

Southwark where bus rides and car-lengths were the usual guide to size.

Against all his own wishes, Atkins was forced to ask a further question.

"Why," he asked Pointer, "are you bothering with any of this?"

(The unspoken bewilderment: houses big enough to lose guns in, acres big enough for bus rides – and yours, all yours. Atkins had no conception, no knowledge of this. Could only ask his question and wait.)

Pointer shook his head, blushed further. "I think it's quite exciting," he said.

There was nothing more any of them could say. No one wanted to underline the statement; no one dared comment. No one missed what it implied, what weakness it lent them all. They rehearsed timidly, without conviction. They went home early and did not drink.

And the next day there was the raid itself.

A fine, early summer day. A Tuesday, and Atkins woke to the sound of his mother hoovering the living-room carpet. A familiar sound, like the perpetual but unacknowledged hum of traffic in the filthy London streets outside.

For the first time in many years Atkins faced a day which held a real and frightening purpose. He shaved quickly and badly, hardly touched his breakfast and told his parents (though they did not ask) that he would be busy today.

"I've got friends to see," he said. "We're going out for the day."

His mother said that was nice, his father said nothing at all and Atkins regretted this – somehow wanted them to know that something important was happening. Today mattered. Details like breakfast and the weather and the sound of a hoovered carpet were at last merely parts of a background; they were insignificant.

Taking the hammer and the replica guns out of the house caused him some difficulty. He had to borrow brown paper and string from his mother, which meant a lie that took ten minutes to prepare – "I borrowed a Bullworker off Reg," he said. "I've got to take it back." His mother, who did not know what a Bullworker was, found the paper and string and handed it over in silence. Then he had to carry the fourteen-pound hammer wrapped up in brown paper as if it was something light; when people saw him on the steps outside he tried to make the parcel look unimportant: he swung it carelessly though his fingers ached.

He called at Daley's place and spent the morning there. In the afternoon they went shopping and amidst frightened, sniggered jokes tried to buy stockings from which to make masks. They could only find tights which made Atkins absurdly angry. In the end they bought two cravats which they hoped to wear cowboy-style, just beneath the eyes.

Lunch was a cold hamburger from a stall near a pub they knew. The sun shone, the onions at least smelt delicious. Chewing, standing on the street by the endless traffic, Atkins felt glad to have his friend with him. There was no question or doubt from Reg. Atkins tried to express his gratitude but found it hard.

"All right, mate?"

Then,

"You just wait. Eh?"

Then other bland words.

Atkins did not know whether or not his friend recognized these tokens; he was not even clear himself why he offered them, just knew that they were part of the change, part of this new feeling. It was a strange day.

At four-fifteen they returned to Daley's house and emptied their pockets – taking only enough money for the train fare. They wrapped the replica guns inside the cravats and put the bundle into a shopping bag, which Reg Daley carried. Atkins hugged the hammer in its brown paper wrapping.

They took the underground to Victoria Station which was crowded with young foreigners among whom policeman occasionally paced. Atkins said little now, was too nervous. The first of the commuter-rush was beginning as they caught their train and the two of them had to stand in the baggage compartment among men in suits for whom Atkins felt the usual, confused stabs of envy and contempt; the secret knowledge which he held though, the power that was unfolding at his hands, kept a smile on his heavy lips. He stared out of the dirty window, craning his neck to see the fields and car-parks go by, considered the thrill of fear he felt, wondered if this was a weakness.

They got off at Three Bridges, Crawley, a small but busy station on the outskirts of the town, and Harold Pointer and Peter Davies were waiting for them with the Austin Maxi. Atkins got in without a word. The very fact that this connection had worked made him feel serious and yet elated. He was now under a little more control, believing that at last things had begun.

It was six-forty-five. The sky was by now a little overcast with fine white clouds but it was still warm. The roads were crowded.

Pointer drove, moving off into the traffic without asking for directions because this had already been settled. After some seconds of uneasy silence he said, "All right?"

"Yeah," said Atkins.

Davies, sitting in the front passenger seat, turned round. He seemed very nervous and his round face was even paler than usual.

"We'll just drive past the once?" he said.

Atkins nodded but said nothing.

"Then you'll drop me off?"

Again, the silent nod.

Davies hesitated, seemed to want to say something else, but then just turned back quickly and stared out of the windscreen at the car in front.

They found the industrial estate, turned into the service road, and quite slowly drove past the entrance to the cash and carry store. During this period, Davies kept his face turned inwards to the car and issued a series of rapid reminders: "Can you see the blue door? Just in the corner where the two walls meet. That's it. The exit to the right of that is where you'll go out. Go a bit faster, Harry ... "

Then they were past. They took the next turning right and located the route back to the motorway.

At last, they drove to Davies's home and he got out hurriedly, almost in relief.

Leaning back in, one hand on the roof, one on the open door, he stared at Atkins for one hesitant moment.

"You reckon it'll be all right?" he asked at last.

"Yeah."

"You don't think – "

"Piss off."

It was a sharp, angry order. Davies was hurt by it and he shut the door slowly, anxious not to slam it in case this caused further annoyance. Inside the car, Pointer said, "Car-park?"

"Yes," said Atkins.

As they drove off, no one turned to look at Davies; it was as if he no longer mattered, was not a part of them any more, had no claim to the fear which bound them in silence.

At the car-park, as planned, they stopped and talked through the plan for the last time. Pointer said that the shotgun was in the boot and this made Atkins angry again.

"What the fuck's the use of that?" he demanded.

Pointer looked bewildered.

"I can get it out again," he said.

"While everyone's looking?"

"I can do it just before we go."

"You stupid bastard."

Silence again. And after a short while, Atkins snapped, "Well go on then."

Using his jacket as covering, Pointer went round to the boot of the car and clumsily removed the shotgun. At one point the coat slipped and the barrel could be clearly seen. Atkins shouted, "For Christ's sake ... "

The tension was very high. When the weapon was at last inside the car, lying across their knees, it seemed the most frightening, most important object any of them had seen. Daley particularly was entranced, noticeably so.

"It's already loaded," said Pointer. He spoke very quietly. He wouldn't meet the eyes of the other two men, yet he seemed quite calm.

"How do you cock it?" asked Atkins.

"Like this – "

Pointer leaned over but Atkins knocked his hand away and said, "Just tell us."

"You pull back the hammers. It won't fire otherwise. It's very old."

"Reg can take it."

"What?"

"Reg can take it. You have his pistol."

This last-minute change of plan seemed to disturb Pointer but he made no comment, simply took and pocketed the replica, which was quickly handed over the top of the seat by Daley.

Atkins had made the change because he guessed that it would please his friend and for no other reason. Watching the mute take and hold the stock of the shotgun he felt glad that it was in his power to make such gestures.

They checked their other equipment: the scarves, the hammer, the Blu-tack and white card for the number plates. They put on gloves. They waited. Some cars were driven away nearby. There seemed a possibility of rain because the clouds had subtly thickened. No one mentioned this or said a word. Atkins no longer wanted to rob the cash and carry store. He was badly frightened. He had taken his plan to the point of execution and each detail had changed his perception by one further degree. There was nothing left of his dream now, simply a reality which oppressed, which waited to spring.

At five to eight he said, "All right. Come on, let's go."

Pointer started the car at once. Then he turned in his seat and said, "I thought you wanted to drive."

"Come *on!*" shouted Atkins.

Pointer turned back and the car moved off. Atkins had forgotten that he was to drive. He sat perfectly still in the back and stared out at the road. He was not able to think clearly. In a strange way, he wanted to cry.

Reg Daley looked at his friend and began to fidget in his seat. He kept touching the shotgun, which lay across them like a snake.

Harold Pointer drove carefully and well. His clothes, Atkins noticed at last, were far too bright really. It was stupid. It was all stupid.

The industrial estate was empty, as Davies said it would be. They stopped the car fifty yards from the entrance to the store, just before a sharp bend.

As soon as they came to a halt, Pointer got out and fixed the white card to the front and rear number plates. It took only a few seconds and when he got back in he took a stitched nylon mask from the dashboard locker and lowered his head to put it on. Doing this, he noticed that Atkins had not moved.

He stared, opened his mouth to speak but said nothing. He lowered the mask and sat still.

It was now four minutes past eight. The car engine continued to run.

Daley and Pointer still watched Atkins, who appeared to stare at nothing and gave no sign of wanting to move. Perhaps it was the shotgun. Perhaps the bright clothes. Or something he had not thought of. Something stupid. Atkins was waiting to call off the robbery and they were aware of this.

Outside the car it was a warm, light evening in which rain was possible. There was no traffic in the estate though there were several parked cars and, in one yard, the trailer of a lorry stood waiting for collection. Atkins neither moved his head nor eyes. His lips were inevitably parted. The problem was that he wanted someone to give him an excuse. Without knowing it, this was all that he wanted. At this moment a single word or gesture would have halted the robbery. It would not have happened.

Pointer, who had wanted only excitement, said, "Come on," in the calmest possible way. He was not excited at all. He was frightened but committed.

Atkins took out the cravat he had bought that morning and said, "Put your masks on."

The pause, the hesitation, was over. They were about to turn their clumsy, irrational dream into a form of reality Atkins at heart dreaded.

He had a little trouble knotting the cravat and Reg Daley helped him. It felt tight across his nose and it was a little difficult to breathe with the thick smell of new cloth in the mouth. Pointer, in the nylon mask, looked very frightening: his face was distorted. It was obscene. Daley's eyes were tremendously bright over his own cravat. He now hugged the shotgun. Atkins felt for his own replica pistol and could not decide whether he should carry it or keep it in his pocket. As he also had the hammer, he put the pistol in his belt just as Pointer put the car into gear and moved off. Pointer drove slowly. They turned the sharp bend and found the entrance to the cash and carry store.

What made Atkins laugh at this moment was the fact that Pointer signalled left as he carefully swung the car in off the road. This seemed so unnecessary. So fantastic.

He said, "Here we go then."

He choked a little on saliva as he said the words and had to swallow quickly. As a result his statement sounded foolish.

The robbery was about to begin. He could not believe it.

Sixteen

Kind began talking to the young man with the pistol, attempting to sound casual while at the same time trying to hurry each sentence because the seconds were important. He stayed leaning forward on the couch as he spoke, elbows on knees so that it would take only a little effort to stand. When he spoke it was in a calm way.

"I don't suppose you'd let my wife go upstairs now, would you?"

"I'm sorry, I can't. The boy's quiet now anyway." Soft reply.

"I know," said Kind, "but it would make us both happier if we could just see for ourselves."

The young man shook his head. He held the pistol diffidently between two hands, not pointing it at anyone, hardly keeping a finger on the trigger.

Kind tried to keep his voice calm, tried to be friendly.

"Is it important that you stay?"

"What do you mean?"

"Must you stay here? Would you lose very much if you just walked out?"

The man appeared to smile at himself, to reflect upon his answer before giving it. Then he nodded. "Yes," he said quietly, "I'd probably lose an awful lot if I just walked out."

"Money, I presume."

"Not money."

"What then?"

"I think you'd better not ask me any more."

"You're frightened your friend might come back?"

A blank, unaccusing face turned towards Kind.

Kind shrugged. He said, "Listen – " And as he said the word he stood up easily, waving his hands as if the whole performance was intended to lend importance to what he was saying. The pistol turned a little towards him but he ignored it and stood quite still, speaking intently but using his hands for emphasis. " – my car's in the garage outside; the key's hanging up in the kitchen. Why don't you – or you and your friend – just take it and drive away?"

"Where to?"

A calm, almost hopeless question which nearly touched Kind, but he was too wound up for this form of sensitivity now, too firmly launched on what he had planned. Time was passing so quickly and this too affected him. Made his words more intense, his gestures more violent.

"Anywhere you like. Go to the coast – take a ferry somewhere. Gatwick Airport's only fifteen miles down the road – "

"I haven't any money. None of us have. Anyway – "

"How much do you need?"

"It's not the point."

"Well what is the point? If you stay here you know what'll happen, don't you? You do know, don't you?"

"Nothing will happen. We'll just go, that's all. As soon as we find out that it's safe to go home."

"Your friend won't let you do that."

"Do what?"

"Just walk out. We've seen your faces – we know that one of you's a mute."

Silence.

"You realize what that means?"

A shaken head. Eyes lowered away from his. Kind saw that Jo was watching him now and he tried to pull her into the conversation, to spread the words so that they were all joined by them, might become comfortable within their framework.

"You tell him, Jo," he said. "Tell him what you're frightened will happen to Danny. Go on."

Jo continued to stare at him as if in disbelief, or as if not trusting him. He said again, "Go on – tell him."

She shook her head and refused to answer. Kind saw the fear in her eyes and looked quickly at the other man to check that he, too, was watching. The young man's eyes were fixed on Jo and he was frowning slightly, seemed embarrassed by the confrontation between husband and wife and by his own part in it.

Kind said, "Anyway. You do know. You know what your friend wants to do."

How long had passed? How much time had he left? Kind began to speak quickly, almost gabbling his words, unsure now whether he intended them simply to bring the other man closer to him or as a real plea, something which might take away the need for what he planned.

"If you just left here now with your friend I could just take my wife and child and walk out and not bother to call the police for an hour. You'd have as much time as you needed to get clear. We'd be safe and you wouldn't be trapped into something you didn't want to do. We'd still be alive and you wouldn't have murder on your hands – "

"Stop it!"

It was Jo. Shouting out loud, bringing all her fears and

tension to the surface at last in a single cry which ended his speech in an instant. It was a powerful sound. The two words possessed both misery and terror; they were an explosion, an outlet. They did not plead but only stated a fact: Jo hated her husband at that second – he felt it. Saw the fierce release.

The sudden anticlimax of the pause which followed was a tired, hopeless moment. There could be nothing but dejection, nothing but a resignation, a giving-up.

Kind let this feeling hang over them for some seconds, let it bathe them in unpleasantness so that they all ached for some change, some diversion. Then, when he judged that these feelings were at their keenest, using that sensitivity which made him a good or bad writer, he said carelessly, "I see. I'm sorry." He sighed. Turned as if thoughtlessly towards the young man with the pistol and went on, "Well I'd like to go the toilet please. Is that permitted?"

"You ought to wait."

"Oh for Christ's sake … "

Gentle exasperation in the tone. Then, slowly and with despairing patience, "I only want to go to the toilet. Please."

It was emotional pressure of the type Kind understood quite well. He had used it in many stories, particularly in those based on the slight, shifting emphasis of subdued arguments – husband and wife rows which simmered and expressed themselves in other ways than shouts and clean breaks. He understood these feelings.

The young man said, "Go on. Please remember … " His voice ended just before the threat he had no wish to utter.

Kind said, "Yes."

He walked past the young man quite slowly, noting that there was no turning of the head to watch his departure, no care at all. This man was outdistanced by his own emotions, was crippled by their pace and could barely now summon the effort to keep his gun trained upwards and not down, dejectedly, towards the floor.

Kind paused just for one small part of a second. He watched the still form of the young man, took in the specks of colour in his clothes, the thinness of the neck where the collar fell away and the gentle brown skin swooped down to the throat and shoulders. He was not a powerful figure at all. And should it be now?

As if sensing, but not seeing, Kind's pause, the young man finally turned. But by the time he faced the doorway Kind had left and there was no confrontation. This had not been the moment but was about to be. Kind paused in the hall and stared at the front door, still latched so that a single pull would open it.

He could run out now. Could alert the neighbours, could make the telephone call which would bring the police. The young guard was so inexperienced, so silly and so polite that this had not occurred to him: the simple pressure of Kind's demand – for Christ's sake, just the toilet – had made him blind to suspicions of escape. How foolish. How unbelievable. Kind, pausing so that the moment became quite dangerous, thought through the likely outcome of his escape: the discovery, Atkins's inevitable return before the police could arrive, the panic of the young man losing unaccustomed power ...

In guilty surprise, Kind recognized that he was forcing this logic on himself, that the points occurred not naturally but in a false way in which the ultimate object was partially concealed from himself – but only partially, because on recognizing the falsehood of his own thoughts the object at once became clearer. He did not want to escape. This was not the outcome he sought. Somehow, in the course of the last four hours he had summoned up a kind of hated for these men – or perhaps, if not hatred, then a fear which must be expunged, must be purged.

Kind thought he understood what had happened to him but realized that the full words would take much time to arrive, that meanwhile he must make do with the taste of feelings.

He passed the front door, pushed his way into the bathroom and closed and bolted the door behind him.

Here, to the left, was a large wall mirror, wide enough to show his head and shoulders. Kind stared at his own eyes, and it was as though this was a person he had reason to understand and yet could not, could not quite yet. There was a little white mucus in the corners of his eyes – this tended to form when he sweated a lot under still conditions. He found it unpleasant and hurriedly wiped it away. He recognized that he was beginning to look a little old, that the flesh of his face was not nearly so firm, so irreducibly fresh as he had once imagined. He remembered America and the miles in the crowded minibus – the people, the young people. They did not write now. Letters were long dead – yellowed things in the drawers somewhere upstairs. Not often read now because of some regret, some dread of nostalgia. Those faces would also be ageing. Kind felt sad about this.

He did not go to the toilet. He waited for perhaps fifteen seconds and then pulled the flush. While the water gushed down into the bowl he turned on the cold tap and let it run for a time. As this happened he reached behind into his belt and took out the paper-knife which was sticking to his hot, damp flesh. It was a relief to be without the pressure of it constantly causing something just under pain.

Kind held it in his hand. He gripped it several ways, trying to decide which might cause his fingers to slip striking, which might be safest – deciding that his hand should be as far up the shaft as possible, so that the flat triangle of the blade provided a stop, a hilt.

How did one use a knife?

He considered this briefly, with a vague disdain.

In the back the ribs were close together and the point might slip or break; yet he must be quick, there could be no time for sound or error. Perhaps a scream. Under the rib-cage, at the back perhaps. Or possibly into the throat striking backwards to where he had seen the soft flesh become lost in an open shirt collar.

The flush had stopped running. There was no need for further pretence. Kind turned off the cold tap and walked to the bathroom door where he hesitated, thought, and placed the paper-knife in his right-hand trouser pocket.

The handle was just a little too long and two inches of it could be seen above the cloth, so Kind kept his hand on it casually, as if this was a natural thing that might be done – walk into a room with hand loosely in pocket.

He knew that there was very little time left now. He opened the door and walked out into the hall, coughing as he went so that the man in the lounge would have no reason to think that he was trying to enter unobserved. There must be no fear, no cause for suspicion.

Seventeen

Ironically, the reality which Atkins had feared so much in the approaching moments of the robbery seemed quite unreal during the event itself. The incidents and problems came one by one and seemed disjointed, not a part of some whole scheme at all. At times he found it difficult to remember what should come next, though it was mostly his own plan and he had forced the others to rehearse it with him many times. There was an absence of real urgency. A stilted progression of details which left him without much grasp on their importance.

They drove up to the blue side-door with the indicators still signalling left because the self-cancelling device had not worked. Pointer braked slowly and put the handbrake on but left the engine running. It was five minutes past eight and the security van was due at any time within the next ten minutes.

There was a small spy-hole in the top of the blue door but no other mark except a Yale lock just above the handle. Atkins took this in vaguely as they all jumped out of the car. His pistol slipped from his belt and fell to the ground and he had to scrabble for it as the other two men ran forward and began kicking at the door. They did so separately until Atkins, now rising, shouted, "Together! Together!"

The men paused, watched each other, then lifted their feet and kicked almost as one. The door shook but did not give. They did it again but there was still no sign of movement. Then, from behind the door came a frightened shout. A voice called, "What is it? Who's that?"

"Again!" ordered Atkins. He thrust the replica pistol into his pocket and held up the sledge-hammer, standing just behind the other two as they drew back and kicked again. The door shook badly. There were no more shouts from inside.

Atkins called out, "Let me have a go."

But the two men kicked again. This time, a gap appeared in the right-hand side between the door and the jamb. The lock was giving. They kicked again and the door grudgingly opened. There was a small dark corridor beyond and Atkins shouted, "In, in ... " He dropped the hammer and followed the two men as they disappeared into the darkness.

He and Daley turned left, and Atkins sensed rather than saw Pointer running to the right. He heard him shouting, "Where's the ... ?" He did not hear the rest.

Atkins eyes were unused to the gloom after the bright
evening outside and he found it difficult to see much at
first. He made out the end of the corridor and saw Daley
wrenching at a closed door. This was not locked but
because his friend was holding the shotgun it took him a
little time to turn the handle. At last he succeeded and
pulled the door wide so that they could both run
through.

The door opened onto the main store hall and they
were both stunned for a moment by a sense of size. There
were huge shelving systems forty feet and more in height
packed with boxes and bottles. The place was well-lighted
but seemed empty of people. Then Atkins saw a
white-coated figure standing at the end of one of the
alleyways and he dug quickly into his pocket for the pistol
but the man ran behind some shelves.

The glass room was immediately to their left. The lights
were still on inside and two men stood looking out at
Atkins and Daley. They wore suits and their faces showed
that they were frightened. They were standing quite still.
Atkins realized that if the lights were on Pointer had not
cut off the electricity supply. He began to swear, but at
that moment the lights did go off and they were suddenly
in semi-darkness eased only by the reflected glare of
strip-lights elsewhere in the huge store.

Daley was watching Atkins for a signal. He wanted to
know what to do next, and for one second this caused his
friend to become angry. Atkins shouted, "In there you
dope."

He ran forward and tried the half-glazed door but
found it locked. He hesitated, seemed at a loss, but then
turned round and used his elbow on the glass, which
shattered immediately. Atkins half-expected the men
inside the room to snatch at him but they did nothing as
he found the key and turned it. The door opened and the
two of them hurried in. There were no bags on the table.

In semi-darkness, Atkins called out, "Where's the money?"

The men shook their heads very quickly. One of them pointed to the safe and said, "We can't open it."

Atkins shouted again, "Where's the money?"

The man facing him said, "It's in there. In the safe. It's been put away."

"Open it!" Atkins thrust forward his pistol, half turning to Daley for support from the shotgun which was then also levelled at the men.

"We can't!" The man was screaming now. "It's a numbers lock. We can only shut it. We can't open it! We can't do it!"

There were sudden footsteps behind and Atkins glanced round to see Pointer arrive in the doorway. Atkins said, "They say it's in the safe." He did not know what to do.

Pointer shouted, "Leave it! We've been too long!"

Atkins said, "Peter said ... " Then he realized what he was saying and stopped. There was a pause. One of the two suited men was still pointing at the safe but saying nothing.

Atkins hesitated for one moment longer, unsure of himself, not knowing what it was best to do.

Pointer said again, "Come on – leave it!"

Daley was looking at Atkins and, quite obviously, would not move if he was not ordered to do so. He was holding his shotgun too far forward in a way which would have knocked ·him backwards had he fired it. The two men before them looked very frightened.

"All right. Out." Atkins half-whispered the words, but immediately he had said them he was taken by hysteria, by a desperate need to run. There was a scrabble at the door and Pointer was through first, then Atkins and then, finally, Daley.

They ran into the darkness of the corridor in which the

broken door shone like a fire. Out in the daylight they found that nothing had changed. The sledge-hammer still lay where Atkins had dropped it, the car engine was running and the indicators were still signalling left.

They did not say a word. Each man scrambled into the car and Pointer jumped into the driving seat. He drove away while the others were still slamming their doors. He began shouting, "Where to? Where to? ... "

But Atkins could not think clearly. He screamed, "Just drive. Go on, drive!"

Pointer took them out on to the service road, then back onto the main highway without bothering to pause or watch for other cars. But there were none. They hit nothing. At a junction Pointer turned left, then began to drive very fast until Atkins, in a clear moment, said, "Pull in."

"What?"

"Pull in. The number plates."

It was quite a busy road and Pointer refused to stop immediately. Despite more shouts from Atkins he drove on for quarter of a mile until they found a quiet side-turning where they pulled in and he removed the white cards, abandoning them on the roadside.

Back behind the wheel, Pointer swivelled urgently and said, "Now where?"

Atkins was hunched forward, his fists clenched on the back of the seat. He stared out of the window as he thought.

"Your place," he said.

"What?"

"Your place. Your old man's not there ... "

"No, but – "

"There's nowhere else. Go there and we'll think."

"But – "

"Go there!"

Pointer hesitated for a moment longer, but could offer

no other suggestion. He turned back to the steering-wheel and drove off sharply.

After a few minutes Atkins had collected himself enough to order Pointer to slow down a little. It took them half an hour to reach the long, tree-lined drive to Pointer's house and by this time Atkins seemed calmer. He ordered Pointer to hide the car in the garage – a converted barn immediately behind the main house – and slowly led the way inside.

By nine o'clock, as night fell quickly, all three men were seated round the huge kitchen table in Pointer's family home, eating lumps of cheese on slices of unbuttered bread. No one was hungry but Atkins wanted something to do so they ate. The only alcohol in the house was gin which they sipped but did not like. None of them had any idea of what they should do next and at first they said very little, each man merely staring at nothing, chewing grudgingly, lost in personal thoughts.

After a while, Atkins said, "We ought to listen to the news."

There was a silence. Then he said, "We've missed it."

Pointer asked what they were going to do and Atkins said just wait. It got dark outside and they still sat there. The house was as large as Pointer had implied and the size of it, and its displays of taste, made Atkins and Daley feel subdued. They did not want to move from the table but knew they would have to, that something ought to be done very soon. No one said a word about the attempted robbery until Atkins remembered a mistake he had made during the scrabble at the end. He swore, and Pointer looked up as if frightened.

"What is it?" he asked.

"I just remembered."

"What?"

Atkins lowered his face into his hands and spoke in a

muffled, hidden way. "I shouted 'Peter said … ' when I was in the office."

"Jesus Christ." The soft, amazed expression was crueler than any insult.

"I didn't mean to," snapped Atkins, looking up sharply. "I just said it. Anyway there are thousands of Peters around … "

His voice faded into uncertainty and his anger failed with it. He looked to Daley for support but found nothing there except averted eyes – a curious, almost sulking air.

"It could have been anybody," said Atkins.

"They'll find us."

"They won't."

"Christ, I don't want to go to jail."

Pointer's sharp, almost tearful cry made Atkins and Daley stare. Atkins knew that he ought to feel contempt for this weakness but did not – he could not even comment on it. He understood what Pointer was feeling and it made him frightened again, made him stand and draw the curtains in complete silence because he did not like the sight of dark windows and black, silent trees in the distant grounds. The sense of strangeness returned to Atkins and when he spoke again it was with an almost hesitant voice.

"What we've got to do," he said, "is find out if they know which Peter it was."

"Yes." Pointer's voice was also quiet, almost a whisper. He did not look up.

"Which means we've got to ring him up," said Atkins.

A pause then. No one wanted to do it. Daley could not, Pointer would not even raise his head. He just said, "What will you say?"

"I don't know. We could ask for Peter and … "

"What if they ask who you are?"

"Put the phone down."

"He might not know anything yet. They might not have worked it out. We don't even know if we can trust him for God's sake."

Silence fell.

Then Pointer, still speaking with quiet anguish, said, "You can't keep ringing."

Atkins shrugged, seemed to hesitate and then sat back down at the table and all three men resumed their staring silences. After a long time Atkins started the argument again and this time it went on for an hour, by which time they could only agree that it was too late to do anything that night and the question of who called Davies and what should be said ought to be put by until morning.

Quietly, Pointer fetched some blankets for the other two and they all went to bed.

Just before they did so, Atkins remembered something else he had said during the raid.

On the landing of that large, half-darkened house he paused and called out to Daley as he was going into one of the bedrooms. Daley paused almost reluctantly and looked over to where Atkins was standing.

Atkins said, "I'm sorry about calling you a dope."

Saying it, he felt embarrassed because the apology sounded stupid. His friend shrugged as if it was not important and disappeared into the bedroom. Atkins, standing alone again, listened to the rural silence of the house and watched the broken ends of his own dreams dance mockingly in the shadows.

Eighteen

When Richard Kind walked back into the lounge with his hand on the hidden paper-knife the young gunman seated at the tabe was talking to Jo.

He was leaning forward over the table with his elbows on the wood and the pistol lying just in front of his hands.

He was saying, " ... I don't know why. We just made too much of it ... "

His back was to Kind. The difficulty was that in the last few seconds he had changed his position so that the wooden back of his chair was directly behind him. Before, he had been sitting sideways on. Now, the chair protected his back. Kind felt very frightened, almost as much as when he had tried to throw coffee at the mute and failed.

The man had short, neat hair. The collar of his shirt was a little dirty around the rim at the back and this absorbed Kind's attention; had it been one of the other two men he would not have been surprised but a dirty collar seemed out of place on this person. He would not be able to stab him through the chair. He would have to attack the side of the neck.

Kind took out the paper-knife and felt both foolish and hideous. The weapon now seemed very small and yet somehow clumsy. He raised it a little, for no purpose other than to increase the pace of events. To raise the knife seemed a beginning. Jo saw. Kind looked across and noted that her face expressed bewilderment. The young gunman must also have noticed this because he turned very quickly while Kind was still three feet from him.

This then happened.

The young man began to scrabble to his feet in an almost hysterical way. His pistol was in his hand but he did not try to use it. Kind stepped forward and tried to grab the gun with his left hand but the man extended both arms until they were perfectly straight and attempted to hold off the paper-knife. His mouth was open but he was silent. He moved his arms like sticks, in a quick, imprecise way. Then he started to shout, "Don't ... don't ... "

The words were not clear, as if he had no time to speak properly.

Kind found that he could hardly move the paper-knife because the pistol was against his hand. He ran forward a little, which caused the other man to stumble and, in a loose knot, they moved past Jo who began to stand and shout, "Leave it! Stop it!"

In running backwards the young man tripped a little and this made him jerk both his hands outwards in an instinctive gesture of balance.

Kind chose the stomach area in a blind way and pushed the knife forward and then realized with delayed amazement that it had entered the man's body. It had taken much less force than he had expected. Also, the knife was now so far into the flesh that the small triangle he had used as a hilt was concealed. Kind felt his thumb against the man. He withdrew the knife and this was a little more difficult.

The man said, "Oh" in a lost way.

Jo made a noise in her throat.

Kind realized that there was blood on the knife. He wanted to clean it. The young man now dropped his pistol which landed with a dull noise on the carpet. He put his hands to the place where the paper-knife had entered him, and began to bend forward. Then he sat down very hard on the floor, quite suddenly. He hugged himself in a hunched way. He did not say anything. He stared at Kind's legs and breathed through an open mouth.

Jo shrieked one word. "Christ!"

It was so loud that Kind flinched away and also there was a responding noise from upstairs in Daniel's room: a brief scrabbling and a door opening quickly. Now there was the heavy sound of feet on the landing.

Kind snatched up the pistol, taking it away from the wounded man as if frightened that he might want to use it though he was not capable of doing so. Trembling, Kind moved the pistol from his left to his right hand, changing it over with the paper-knife which clattered against the barrel. He did not know how to use a pistol. He believed that some, perhaps all, had safety-catches. He was frightened that the catch on this weapon might be on.

Daley was now running down the stairs.

Kind could not find a safety-catch. He said, "Oh, oh." It was a foolish, frightened sound. His wife had her hand to her open mouth and was staring at the young man on the floor. She seemed unable to move or speak, seemed unaware, after her shouted cry, of what was happening. The man on the floor began to bend further forward, still holding the wound. Now blood could be seen through his jumper.

Daley must have jumped the last few stairs because there was a loud sound on the hall floor which made Kind look up. So that when the man appeared in the doorway, pointing his shotgun towards the ceiling, their eyes met at once.

There was the slightest hesitation as the mute looked at his fallen friend and took in as much as he was able to of what had happened.

Kind pointed the pistol at the man and pulled the trigger. His eyes were partly closed in anticipation of the noise and he held his face away slightly. There was only a clicking sound. Kind pulled the trigger again.

Daley now pointed his loaded shotgun at Kind and pulled at the trigger, but was unable to fire it. He continued to try in the second or so it took Kind to understand that his own weapon was of no use.

Jo began screaming, "No! No! No! ... "

This was a deadening noise.

Kind watched the mute begin to tear at the hammers of the shotgun. He dropped his pistol and ran forward in a frantic, ungainly way.

Seeing Kind's rush, the mute tried to back away, pulling up the barrel of the shotgun so that it could not be grabbed. Kind pushed at him with his right hand and because he was so much heavier the two of them fell back against the wall. Kind pushed at the man with the paper-knife. It was in his left hand which meant a poor angle so the knife failed to penetrate. Jo was now running forward at the two men, still shouting and screaming. Kind felt her hands on him but did not know what it was.

He drew the knife back and stabbed forward again a number of times. The mute made a tearing sound in his throat and began falling. Kind felt the weight on his hands and stepped back, then he had to step back still further because the man fell on him. He almost tripped over Jo and there was a brief struggle for balance as they watched Daley fall forward over his shotgun and lie still.

Kind was breathing very heavily.

Jo said, "What have you done? What have you done?"

Kind tried to find words and realized that he was still holding the paper-knife, which he then dropped.

He turned back to the other young man and saw that he was still bent forward, still holding his stomach. This man was beginning to cry or groan very quietly. His face was perhaps one foot from the floor, facing it intently.

Kind looked back at the mute but he had not moved, did not do so.

Kind said, "It was Danny. Danny's upstairs. There were two of them … "

Jo knelt down and touched the man who lay at their feet. She began to say that he was dead but Kind did not hear because he was still speaking. He shut his eyes then, screwed up his face very tightly and opened them again. Jo was looking up at him.

"I'll call the police," said Kind.

"Call an ambulance!" Jo shouted. "Get a fucking ambulance!"

"I'll call the police. They can call an ambulance."

Kind had to step over the fallen man to get out of the lounge and he hesitated to do so, touched by a feeling of indelicacy. There was no other way though and eventually he straddled the figure, stumbling a little on the butt of the shotgun which lay under the body.

Outside in the hall he coughed and swallowed. He could hear the other young man's cries beginning to become clearer for a moment, more anguished. It was a disturbing sound. Through the window on the stairs Kind could see a young girl ride by on a pony. She was riding on the grass and he could not hear the sound of the hooves.

He walked into the kitchen and remembered then that the telephone was broken, had been destroyed by Atkins only a short time before. Kind had forgotten this and now he stood indecisively for a moment. Without turning round he called out, "The phone's broken." Then he said, "You ought to look at Daniel."

Jo said nothing and Kind said, "Jo?"

He heard her shout back, "For Christ's sake!"

At that moment the front door was pushed open and Atkins walked into the hall and stood looking at Kind.

Nineteen

Atkins was woken up by a rough shaking and the sound of a fierce whisper which only gradually became comprehensible.

" ... moving about and there's nothing there, it shouldn't ... "

"What ... ? What ... ?"

Slowly, as Atkins sat up in bed and took in Pointer's

pale, frightened face, he understood what it was the man ways saying: there was movement outside; there were lights in the grounds.

Atkins rose and stood at the dark window, side by side with Pointer who continued to whisper for a moment in a badly scared way, "I was just going to the toilet and I saw it moving. Just to the left of the main drive, in the trees … "

They stood there for some minutes while the full power of Pointer's fear took over and also controlled Atkins. They waited in silence, staring out into the black ramble of grounds which surrounded the huge house. From time to time Pointer broke the silence to whisper, "Wait – wait … "

And then at last he said, "There!"

With a tremble of terror, Atkins saw a single light moving among trees or bushes a hundred yards away. The light flickered briefly and then went out. He waited for it to come again but nothing happened. He said, "What is it?" Barely a whisper. Hardly any strength at all left in his body.

"I don't know," said Pointer. "It shouldn't be there. There shouldn't be anyone … "

"What's down there?"

"Nothing. Trees."

"Trees?" Atkins wanted to know what time it was but did not dare ask. Neither man had to explain their fears because it was quite clear what both believed.

"Quickly," Atkins whispered. "Wake up Reg and get downstairs." He thought for a moment longer, holding the other man with him by clamping a hand on his shoulder. "No lights," he said at last. "No sound. We've got to go. Get the car."

"What?" Pointer seemed incredulous, but Atkins had by now mustered all that power of fantasy which lay in years behind him. Fantasy was a power, a weapon.

"Move!" he said. And he went to get dressed in the mild summer darkness.

From this moment there were no queries to the decisions Atkins made. In the kitchen he ordered the other two to follow him quietly, half crouching, out of the back door and over to the garage. With aching care, Atkins undid the rusting bolt which held the double doors together and they crept inside. The place smelt of oil and rust. The Austin Maxi was like another member of the gang and they crept to it like children.

"Get in ... " Atkins's whisper was unnecessary. All three men opened silent doors and slid onto the plastic seating. This time, Pointer did not attempt to take the wheel but sat in the back and seemed glad to be there, as if this was somehow a safer place to be. With a hissed order, Atkins demanded the key and then paused for one second before turning on the ignition.

Almost with bravado he said, "Here goes ... " And he turned the key, the engine fired and he switched on the lights at the same time. A shock. It seemed a vast noise, a brilliant light.

But then Atkins had found the gear and they were out, speeding down the white glared drive, each man waiting for the sudden shout, the other cars, the dark forms emerging from bushes and trees ...

They made it to the gate and plunged through, swerving to the right into the small side lane.

They did not say a word. They were all watching for the slightest movement.

Atkins drove far too fast for the bumpy lane and the car bounced roughly as they sped over the stones and pot-holes. The lane was only a hundred yards long and they made it to the main road in a few seconds. Still no obstruction, no movement to stop them. Atkins began to feel very brave and he acclerated so quickly that the tyres squealed on the tarmac. They had escaped.

Minutes later, still speeding north on deserted roads, Atkins asked what time it was.

"Three-thirty," said Pointer. "What are we going to do?"

The question thrilled Atkins because it delegated authority; the raid might have failed but the escape might succeed. The surge of pleasure stayed with him for the next ten minutes and he did not even bother to consider answering the question until he had found a side lane, turned in, and then switched off the engine.

Speaking into the darkness he said, "Well – as I see it, that may or may not have been the law."

He was almost laughing.

Pointer nodded and watched his half-hidden face. Daley, still hugging the shotgun which he had refused to abandon, looked badly frightened and made small noises in his throat.

"Don't worry, Reg," said Atkins, "we'll see nothing happens to you."

This brought one brief, nervous smile.

Atkins went on, "If it *was* the law then we've got to get away from here because that Davies bastard must have talked and they know who we are. Right?"

"Yes." Pointer spoke quietly but anxiously.

"But if it *wasn't* the law, then we're all right. Or we should be."

"Yes … " More doubtfully now.

Atkins paused. Pinned down to the point of conclusion by his own logic he now realized that he had no answer, that either possibility defeated him: if the police were aware of their identities, then, as he said, they must get away – but to where? And how? But again, if the police did not know, how were they going to check?

Atkins turned away from his men and stared out of the windscreen at the dark, shifting branches of summer trees which hung over the car. It was not like Southwark. He felt in the wilderness here; there was too much silence, too many secret corners of countryside. He hated it. Shifted restlessly in his seat and tried to face the problems he had outlined, but could not.

Three-forty-five in the morning. Atkins felt – no, *knew* – that safety would vanish with the arrival of daylight. He must have an answer, wanted desperately to lead yet had nowhere to take his men. Had no direction yet. It seemed unfair, frightening and hopeless.

"First thing," he said at last, "is to get yours heads down and get some sleep. We can't do anything till morning. We'll settle it then. All right?"

He was defiant now, seeking nothing but agreement and he received this from the men on the back seat though in a reluctant way. Atkins wanted Reg to talk to, wished for the first time that his friend could speak. He had nothing to say to Pointer.

Settling down to sleep, uncomfortable and curled up like a child, Atkins stared into the foreign darkness of the car and fought a feeling of extreme loneliness. After a while he said, "All right, Reg?"

There came a small sound from the back, then silence. Atkins recognized the sound, understood what it meant, and smiled. Eventually, he did sleep.

The rest of the night passed in a cramped, aching way, broken by the shifting of tired bodies and the occasional burst of headlights streaming onto the overhead trees from the Brighton road nearby. Atkins was fully awake by seven but pretended to sleep on for another hour while he resumed his struggle to find some way through the mess which had been created out of his dreams.

The problems were mostly of his own making: he had no money, only a little change left over from buying the train tickets; he had no fresh clothes, no transport other than Pointer's car and no way of checking with his parents whether the police had indeed called at his home: neither his parents nor Reg Daley's were on the telephone. He could simply drive back and see, but what if the police were waiting? What if he was caught? Atkins was more frightened of this idea than of anything else in his life. The fear confused him and made it difficult to think clearly. Really, he wanted to be in his bedroom now, to be leading the gang from there, briefing them perhaps, again and again. That had been good. There had been some point to that. But this ... ?

By eight o'clock the sun was bright enough to ruin any pretence of sleep, so he sat up and rubbed his eyes. As he took away his hands and sight returned, Atkins had a frightening impression of vulnerability: daylight did this to him. There was a low hedge and then green fields; there were trees; in the distance behind there was the clear sound of cars. Everything was so – bright, so light. They were exposed, were open to discovery at this minute or this or this.

They must hide. That much he knew.

Also?

Atkins struggled with the thought. Yes, as they had discussed last night, must telephone Davies. See if he was in, ask what was happening. That was the only way. He must telephone Davies.

Atkins turned round to face the tired, pale men in the back seat and said, "Right. The first thing is to bell Peter and ask what's going on."

The others nodded. The car smelt stale. They all wanted to move, to have fresh air coming in through an open window. They all went out to relieve themselves, standing at the roadside with bowed heads like condemned men.

One by one they climbed back in and Atkins started the car, noticing in doing so that the petrol tank was almost empty. He asked if anyone had any money but they had none, only bits of change. Atkins swore and drove off.

He found the main road again and continued north. There was a telephone-box in the small village and at ten past eight Atkins dialled Peter Davies's number but there was no reply. They drove on a little further and found another box. At twenty past eight he dialled again; no reply, the number rang out and out like an unanswered cry for help and when Atkins put the phone down he did it so hard that the box rang metallically, like a huge bell. They parked for a long time, discussed hardly anything and then tried again; there was still no answer.

They drove on a little further and came to a small market town which seemed to be stocked entirely with tidy, middle-class houses and well-planted gardens. Atkins loathed it, began swearing as soon as they touched its rim. He did not know what the town's name was nor care – he possessed a gang and they were bound to him by fear; this much was clear to him. There was still a little glory in these last moments.

They talked about why Davies or his mother had not answered the telephone but could only make endless suggestions – Pointer to Atkins, Atkins to Pointer, Daley watching like a dog ready to follow, nothing to say though.

Atkins said they did not have enough petrol to drive any further and anyway they couldn't just cruise about the open roads like this because someone would spot them. Pointer said nothing at this; was capable of thinking much clearer than Atkins but did not dare, had not the courage for it.

When the car engine misfired, caught again and then died completely it was a moment of almost complete hysteria. They coasted to the kerbside and stopped and the silence was like something final, like a dead thing. There was a naked feeling in the way they could only sit waiting for someone else to suggest something. One by one they were losing their props and now there was almost nothing left.

Pointer summed it up then when he just said quietly, "We can't even afford any petrol."

"Shut up!" Atkins's shout was pointless; was merely a sign of desperation.

In a little while a police car drove slowly past and all three men sat completely still, not daring to meet the faces of the uniformed officer s who turned to watch them as the car cruised alongside and went on – still slowly.

Pointer, whispering, hardly moving his lips, said, "If we stay here we've had it."

Atkins could think of nowhere to go. The police car drove down a small hill and disappeared. When it had gone, Atkins forced himself to say, "Right – we ought to get out."

In the scramble of movement which followed it took a shouted warning from Atkins to remind Daley to hide the shotgun. There was a mackintosh on the back window-ledge and he draped this round the weapon and though it was still an incongruous object it was better than no concealment at all.

Atkins still had no idea where they should go, he only knew that they could not stay on the street and they were miles from anywhere they knew, anywhere safe. They could not even afford to sit in a pub.

The dream-sense, the fantasy, was swelling to encompass him once more like a protector, a friend. A subtle numbness began to dull his feelings and he walked away from the main road and up a small side-street without bothering to look back at, or speak to, his friends. This street seemed slightly untidier than the rest of the town, a little cosier. The dream grew further and Atkins felt more comfortable, more closed in.

After about twenty or thirty paces Harold Pointer called out, "Where are we going?"

It was a pathetic cry, full of childish despair, and it made Atkins smile and stop.

Turning then, he saw a house which looked less intimidating than others they had passed. Small windows at the front, little to see inside; next door, a garage with white doors. Atkins had nothing to say really; he was quite without an idea and yet the others were standing just below him on the small hill, waiting for his words, his orders.

Atkins hesitated, then pointed to the house and said, "In here."

His own words boomed at him, as if in a tunnel or a vast, empty room with invisible sides.

Pointer neither argued nor agreed. Daley really only understood when, standing on the doorstep, he was told to get his shotgun ready. Atkins, hearing the sound of his own knuckles on the wood, hearing the lock turn in an ordinary way, experienced one horrified glimpse of despair which he concealed with the words, "All right, lads. Here we go."

Jo Kind opened the door and they rushed in on her.

Twenty

The return of Greg Atkins and his appearance in the tiny hallway neither surprised nor frightened Kind at first. The event was almost peripheral. So much had happened in the last few seconds that he felt unable to absorb more shocks or attach importance to this new situation.

He did not even bother to speak as the man continued to stare at him in an uncertain way. Kind recognized that this was a new threat but had no idea what to do or say.

Atkins frowned. He opened his mouth and called, "Reg?"

It was a hesitant, questing sound. It worried Kind and

made him step backwards as if expecting a blow or a sudden explosion of anger.

"Reg?" Louder this time. Atkins waited for a second and then changed his shout, calling, "Harry?" in a quick, urgent way.

Kind said, "It's too late ... " But then his voice broke a little and he had to stop, knowing that it was a foolish, weak pause. He tried to speak again but found that he could not, that he was physically unable to say a word just as the dead man in the next room had been.

"What's happened?" said Atkins. "Where are they? What's happened?"

As Kind watched, the man dug into the pocket of his anorak and drew out the pistol, pointing it uncertainly first at Kind and then a little to the left and right as if unsure from which direction an attack might come.

Kind stepped forward, raising a hand, wanting to calm the man, to soothe him before there was any more violence or fury – but in doing so he saw the expression on Atkins's face change utterly in a single glance, and he stopped in sudden bewilderment. He saw that Atkins was staring at his hand. Looking down, Kind found traces of blood on his fingers. He found it a brutal, outlandish sight. Was hardly less fascinated than Atkins himself and felt almost as much incomprehension for this taint, this bright colour.

In that pause, Kind found himself able to speak once more.

He said, in a flat, toneless voice, "I couldn't do anything else."

"Do what?" Atkins was not looking angry at all. He was looking badly frightened, not at all the same person who had ordered Kind into the lounge with sharp, violent gestures only five hours before. This seemed a different man, even with the pistol he seemed quite different. He looked suddenly hunted; swiftly changed like a man who has relied on something which was not there. Kind understood the look, could have explained it in writing, could have eased it convincingly into a story.

Yet Kind did not know how to meet it, not now. Did not know what to risk saying – felt almost embarrassed, called to account for something he did not want to think about.

"Do *what?*" shouted Atkins again.

Jo came out of the lounge very quickly, breaking into the confrontation with barely a glance at her husband.

"Get a doctor," she told Atkins. "Go and use the phone … "

"Why?"

"Call a *doctor*."

Both were near to hysteria. Kind called out, "It's all right, Jo … " But he was ignored. Atkins suddenly pushed Jo to one side and ran into the living-room. Pausing for one moment – almost a coward's moment – Kind heard the single, bewildered sound, "Oh … "

Jo suddenly made for the front door, obviously intent on telephoning for help, but the sight of her starting to leave made Kind cry out, "Wait! Wait a minute!"

Jo turned at the door and he realized that he could not explain why she must stay with him, that it was simply a need not to be left alone now, even though it was best for her to go, best that they should both be clear of all this. Kind felt committed. Sensed that he ought to stay and see through what little of this scene remained. Just a few seconds. He wanted help though, could not do it by himself. Needed Jo to come and stand with him as he tried to find a way across the final distance, managed those last steps which had been eluding him throughout the morning. It was a mixture of foolish bravery and utter cowardice. Kind sensed it but did not understand it at all, not in words; could not touch anything so close, so confusing.

He said, as she watched, "Just a moment. Let's see ... "

See what? He had no idea. Had said anything. Jo seemed to look with hatred at him but that may have been wrong – again, he could no longer tell.

She said, "What for?" But all the same she walked back towards him as Kind stepped out into the hall and followed Atkins into the lounge.

Atkins was staring at his dead friend. He had his back to Harold Pointer, who by now was curled up on the floor like a sleeping child, though soft movements of his shoulders showed that he was not sleeping. It seemed unfair to Kind that Atkins should turn his back on the living; the dead man could surely claim no time now?

Atkins seemed entranced. His thick lips were parted and his pistol hung by his side in an abandoned, forgotten manner.

Kind said, "I didn't mean it."

Didn't mean. He nearly laughed. He stepped forward as if going somewhere positive but then hesitated in an almost decent way. Again, he did not want to step over the body. Felt stupid.

Atkins awoke from the trance at that moment, and as Kind paused, he drew up the pistol and pointed it in a trembling, tearful way. In fact, when he spoke, his voice was also shaking and it seemed that he might soon cry. Kind heard Jo come in behind him and stop in the doorway.

"You ought to put that down," he said.

"You bastard."

"It's silly."

"You've killed him."

"He had a gun."

"You've killed Reg."

Kind watched the trembling pistol and at last found fear again. It was the trembling as much as the weapon itself. It indicated such passion, so much energy waiting to emerge, to express itself.

"He tried to shoot me," he said quickly. "I couldn't do anything else ... "

He was stopped by the fragile, unimportant sound of Atkins's pistol clicking – again, again, again. Atkins was crying now. He was pointing the pistol and pulling uselessly at the toy with ludicrous intensity. It took Kind some seconds to realize that he would not be shot, that there was no danger from this pistol because, like the other one, it would not fire.

He said, "Put it down." He stepped forward across the dead man without a thought, holding out one bloodstained hand in a gentle supplication which drew only a look of agony from the other man.

Atkins did not fire again, merely jumped forward and with a yell of tears beat uselessly at Kind's bulkier figure.

The pistol dropped to the floor. Kind stumbled backwards and smelt the sweat of the man, saw tear-stained cheeks only inches from his own face. He fell into Jo and began trying to shove the hysterical man away from him, aware as he did so that Jo was shouting as she had done before – though it did not matter, was not important.

Now Atkins had dropped to his knees and was scrabbling on the floor. The butt of the shotgun was in his hands and he was levering it upwards, trying to force the body of his friend to one side to get it clear.

Jo was screaming.

Kind shouted, "No ... " He dropped to his knees and began trying to wrestle the weapon away from Atkins. They became entangled in the dead man's arms; prised live fingers away and also the dead.

Atkins was incoherent. He was uttering sharp, grunted noises just as his friend had done. Mute noises. Frightening sounds which made Kind scrabble all the more hysterically for the weapon.

He pulled very hard, felt his own strength at last overcoming the intensity of the other man and with a new effort pulled again.

The barrel of the shotgun flew up and Kind experienced a flash of pain as his left-hand grazed along the smooth steel and encountered the sharp outcrop of hammers.

There was an explosion which seemed to fill the world. It was a feeling, not a noise. A deadness. A sudden and utter interruption which bewildered Kind, left him stunned and frightened.

He realized that his hands were empty, that the shotgun had jumped backwards out of reach and that there was now blood on the white wall just in front of his eyes.

Kind looked to the right and with slow, imprecise vision, took in the fallen form of his wife. She was lying quite still and when Kind stood and went to crouch over her he found that her face had been destroyed and that a part of her head had gone. On the wall opposite there were pieces of flesh and some strands of dark hair.

Kind was unaware of Atkins, who knelt by the body of his friend and hid tear-filled eyes in shock or perhaps terror or sadness.

Kind began shrieking. Crying much harder than Atkins. He started to touch Jo, then drew back, then held there, unsure what to do, what to say. He felt ashamed for not wanting to touch his own wife.

Upstairs, Daniel woke up and began crying. In the lounge, Harold Pointer called out once, softly, as if asking a question.